THE BENGAL TIGER

Studies in Austrian Literature, Culture and Thought

Translation Series

JEANNIE EBNER

THE BENGAL TIGER

Translated and with an Afterword

by

Lowell A. Bangerter

ARIADNE PRESS

Translated from the German *Der Königstiger*,
©1984 Verlag Styria, Graz Wien Köln.

Library of Congress Cataloging-in-Publication Data

Ebner, Jeannie.
 [Königstiger. English]
 The Bengal Tiger / Jeannie Ebner ; translated and with an afterword by Lowell A. Bangerter.
  p. cm. -- (Studies in Austrian literature, culture, and thought. Translation series)
 Translation of: Der Königstiger.
 ISBN 0-929497-54-6
 I. Title. II. Series.
 PT2665.B6K6613 1992
 833'.914--dc20   92-7279
                                                CIP

Cover Design:
Art Director and Designer: George McGinnis

Copyright ©1992
by Ariadne Press
270 Goins Court
Riverside, CA 92507

All rights reserved.
No part of this publication may be reproduced or transmitted
in any form or by any means without formal permission.
Printed in the United States of America.
ISBN 0-929497-54-6

Once again the little boy with the large, bright eyes stood in the gaping crowd before the Bengal tiger's cage.

The animal keeper recognized him immediately. To be sure, his shabby form had the instinctive ability not to attract attention, to disappear in groups of people, to merge with the walls of buildings that he squeezed past, and to glide along as a shadow among shadows when he walked homeward through the streets toward evening. Anyone who did not look into his eyes might easily overlook the boy completely. But the attendant had casually looked into his eyes, and one did not forget them again. Although it was the eyes especially that had attracted the animal keeper's attention, he now noticed that he had not remembered their color correctly, perhaps because until now the boy had always remained in the shadows, while today, on this golden bright, radiant spring day, he stood so that the sun was shining on his face. His eyes were not dark, as the attendant had thought, but yellow. Only the pupils were unusually large, black, glowing points in the borderless circles of the irises.

The attendant dealt more with animals than with people during the largest part of the year—the zoo was flooded with visitors only during the beautiful seasons—and many of the animals had yellow or greenish-yellow eyes, especially the birds and the predatory cats. This color was a rarity in human beings and was bound to attract attention or arouse suspicion, but it would have been ridiculous to want to compare the small, weak child's form with the malice and ferocity of a vulture, wolf, or leopard. There was nothing regal about him; rather he appeared to come from the hordes of barefoot beggar children in the slums. Spontaneously, the attendant thought to himself that this thin lad would probably be content if shelter, food, and care were allocated to him as abundantly as to the Bengal tiger that appeared to interest him so vitally.

He was already considering speaking to the little boy and, if he proved to be unpretentious and likable, taking him along to his quarters between the serpent house and the elephant pen and sharing his meal with him. But the boy was standing too deep in the crowd, wedged into the mass of colorlessly boring zoo visitors who had put on their Sunday clothes to enjoy the first sunshine, the nature park, and incidentally the cheerful feeling that came from the strange, safely controlled creatures that they approached with a certain plebeian arrogance: as masters and mistresses of creation. The attendant did not like to attract the people's attention. In his domain he was the only overseer over a number of beings whose glances and attention hardly took note of him; only under the dull influence of hunger did they notice the food that he brought them, without thanks, joy, or criticism.

He did not like people. They bored him, for they lacked the pronounced diversity that he found in the animals. One like the other, they had two legs, they all walked upright, and their necks were nearly the same length, their skins similar in color and smoothness, their habits, preferences, and opinions quite cut to fit and parallel.

He tried to imagine the pretty woman in the first row of onlookers with motile ears that ended in tufts like those of a lynx. In his thoughts he painted zebra stripes across the bright vest of the plump gentleman next to her. As an experiment, he wished the pink feathers of a flamingo onto the buttocks of a little rosy girl. But then he dismissed this play of his imagination with a dispassionate motion of his hand and rejected his creative mood. All of them, adorned with the manifold splendor of the animals, would make a ridiculous impression at best. Only the little boy had the yellowish green lights of a predator carved diagonally into his flat face without them being detrimental to his appearance.

Soon after that the crowd thinned, disappointed, even somewhat offended because the tiger lay motionless in its enclosure and looked through them with an expressionless gaze. Only the boy remained standing there. The attendant approached him, pointed to the sign on the door of the cage, and, because he presumed that the boy was not yet able to read, explained the inscription to him:

"That is the Bengal tiger," he said.

The boy nodded shyly.

"Are you already familiar with the other animals?" the keeper asked.

"I know all the animals," the boy answered. "From my picture book."

"So, you have a picture book? Well, do you already know how to read?"

"No," said the boy. "My grandmother reads to me."

"Well, what does it say in there about the Bengal tiger?"

The boy moved like a flash, ducked under the barrier chain that forced the people to remain at a safe distance from the cages, and slid along near the iron bars to the other side of the cage.

"I won't tell!" he shouted back scornfully. He bobbed up nimbly on the other side again, and vanished in a crowd of spectators, pushing his way through slick as an eel and with reckless audacity. He acknowledged the indignantly murmured "Well, can't you be careful! What a rascal!" with an apish grimace and then rushed off down the chestnut-lined street, his heels flying, bandy-legged and tiny, but full of energy.

Shaking his head, the attendant turned away.

Children, he thought—children are strange. When they have their favorite snack in their paws, they do not want to give any of it to anyone, and they get angry the moment that you watch them or get too close to them while they chew and suck on it. What could there be in a picture book that is so special that such an urchin does not want to share it with any other person?

Then he forgot the boy until the next Sunday.

But then when he saw him again, standing in front of the Bengal tiger's cage, only occasionally shifting his weight from one thin leg to the other, and staring at the lazy animal for probably an hour, the attendant's curiosity was aroused once more. The little boy's inexplicable stubbornness awakened within him the long-lost desire for nonviolent conquest of alien shyness and wildness.

For the attendant had once been a young animal tamer and had presented a famous trained animal act in a large traveling circus. The peculiarity of his performance had lain in the fact that in a single number he had united different species of animals that were bitterly hostile toward each other in the wild and would have much preferred to eat each other. Besides that, he had entered the arena without whip and prod and had held the animals in check with his glance alone, or at most with his voice by continually talking softly to them. How well he still remembered the extreme exertion that was needed at the slightest trembling of the pelt behind the ears, to direct his gaze and will immediately at the rebellious animal with a concentrated command, without releasing the others even momentarily from the force field of his authority and attention! How exhausting and yet enhancing to his feeling of life it had been to be tiger and antelope, bear and elephant, cobra and vulture at the same time, and many times beyond that: to be the focus, from which will and command radiated irresistibly into their limbs, immobilizing and compelling, domineering and at the same time powerless.

Could he now no longer succeed in taming an unruly guttersnipe?

He waited until about noon, when the crowd's curiosity directed itself toward more peaceful sensations and the people hurried more briskly past the cages toward the restaurant. Then, suddenly ten years younger, his chest puffed up in circuslike pride and muscle-vaunting strength, he approached the boy, keeping his gaze calmly and firmly fixed upon him, and said, "Don't you want to go eat?"

He stretched his hand out toward him. Then something remarkable occurred. Cowering, the little boy slowly and smoothly took two steps backward. His upper lip rose trembling and exposed the small, pointed incisors, and at the same time he gave forth a soft, warning hiss. Then for several seconds he remained tense, defensive, and recalcitrant, with his yellow gaze boring into the attendant's pupils. Suddenly he yielded. His body relaxed. Cringing, he looked away and silently shook his head.

"Do you want to come with me and have coffee and a sandwich?" the animal keeper asked, being careful not to let his words convey any sort of solicitation.

Again a shake of the head, soft, but trembling with secret resistance.

The attendant shrugged his shoulders. "Then don't." And he turned away. He heard a grinding sound behind his back, turned around, and saw the boy kicking up little clouds of dust as he ran away with his heels flying. After he had put some distance between himself and the attendant, which seemed to guarantee him safety, he stopped, turned around, and began to make faces at the animal keeper. He performed a wild ape dance and uttered derisive, half-sung cries. When the attendant neither threatened him with his fist as he had expected, nor made a move to run after him, he lost interest in his challenge. With his hands bored into the baggy pockets of pants that dangled to the hollows of his knees, he sauntered away, stirring up little clouds of dust with his bare toes and whistling shrilly to himself. Suddenly he bent down, picked up a rock, threw it energetically at the wall that surrounded the park, and rushed quick as a flash out the gate.

The attendant was satisfied with the beginning of the taming process, because two hours later the boy was already standing in front of the cage again. Nor had he expected anything else. The fascination that came from the tiger combined effectively with the magic that the attendant had cast over him. The little boy had never before experienced not being beaten when he behaved rudely. His grandmother boxed his ears as a matter of course that had long since become habit, the way you carry out actions that are, to be sure, ineffective but seemingly necessary. She did it without anger, as someone would perhaps strike at a troublesome fly that lands untouched again and again on the pudding. His father usually beat him in advance, for in the boy's mocking, yellowishly glowing glance he saw the will to commit malicious pranks, even before they were carried out, and after they had been carried out anyway, he struck at him again, usually only idly now, and let him slip away, or sometimes did not—that depended on his degree of educative resignation and also on his degree of drunkenness. If he was half drunk, then it could go badly with the lad, but if he was no longer steady enough on his legs, then he made only a few helpless attempts to catch him, and after that he gave up, cursing, with a few vulgar threats for later, which he usually immediately forgot again.

For the boy, both the vain chasing and the beatings were signs of the powerlessness of the adults. They hit him because, as little as he was, they could not cope with him in any other way, not with his wildness and not with his obstinacy. He did not take their blows overly seriously, nor did he take them badly. He despised them. He despised his father without pity, coldly and critically. Some sympathy was mixed in with the contempt for his grandmother.

The picture book, the only plaything that he owned, dated from his grandmother's youth. It was indescribably shabby and dirty, but to him it was a treasure. Now and then he blackmailed his grandmother into reading to him from it, by first behaving noisily and impetuously for half an hour and throwing tantrums in front of the old woman's feet so that she almost fell down, by pinching her and untying her apron strings until she was at her wits' end and decided to rattle off a few of the verses beneath the pictures, simply to keep the little devil quiet for a few minutes.

Of course he long since knew the verses by heart; he only used his blackmail tactics as an excuse to be able to behave like someone possessed before she read to him. Sometimes he immediately snatched the book away from the old woman again and continued to leaf through it by himself. While doing so, he recited the verses aloud or sang them dissonantly to himself. Finally he threw the book into a corner, hastily gave the old woman another shove as he ran past her, and went outside, onto the street or to the zoo.

The zoo and the picture book were strangely but undeniably related to one another, no differently perhaps than dream and reality are connected. In the book there were illustrations of the animals in the zoo, and these animals spoke, not as people usually speak to each other, of course, but in elevated, solemn, and elegant language. They used expressions that the boy had never heard employed by either his grandmother or his father. Thus Mr. Ox might say to his son: "You ruffian, learn fine manners!" While the boy's father at most reprimanded his son for his insolent comments with: "Shut up!"

Originally the boy had believed that the book's creatures were just as contrived and irreal as the words in it, but then he had discovered the zoo and had actually seen these strangely formed beings there, all of them, even the Bengal tiger, his favorite, who, in the picture book, said to a small half-starved, shabby tiger child:

"I am your father, the Bengal tiger!
My realm lies by the Dark Continent's Niger."

The youth had immediately identified with the shabby tiger boy when he stood in front of the cage and met the calm gaze of the old Bengal tiger for the first time. He had tried repeatedly to get this, his silent, powerful, and elegant father to speak, by throwing little rocks into his cage, dancing around in front of the bars, and making faces. For him, the fall and defeat of all of the mighty began with the fact that they could be lured from their restraint by his naughtiness. But the Bengal tiger could not be rattled that easily. It did not make a fool of itself, either by attempting to grab the boy or by striking its paws against the bars of the cage. It did not even roar at him. It rested majestically, full of imperturbable authority, in its inaccessible domain—the Dark Continent, which did not mean anything to the boy. Therefore, that domain stood before his soul, wrapped in a magnificent, mysterious darkness.

Since observing only an impressive calmness with respect to his mischievous pranks in the powerful eyes of the animal keeper as well, the little boy thought that the attendant was also a resident of that invisible Dark Continent. By the Niger? Perhaps the animal keeper was even the Niger in person. He had asked his grandmother who the Niger was. But she had only muttered, "I don't know. That's just what it's called."

The attendant continued his training by frequently fastening his gaze on the little boy, of course, but with a very cool, hypnotic stare, as though he were looking right through him. And beneath that gaze the boy became strangely uncomfortable; a tangible weakening of his brazen self-assurance and self-confidence always came from it. He hoped, half afraid, that the attendant would speak to him again and scold him because of his behavior. But that did not happen, and soon he reached the point of cringing beneath the animal keeper's gaze. He would have liked best to throw himself to the ground and whine softly, but he resisted that senseless and humiliating urge.

One day, late in the afternoon, shortly before the zoo was closed to the visitors, the attendant approached him. The boy stiffened with fear and suspicion and was most inclined to run away, but his thin, bowed legs stood as though riveted to the spot, and he could not even take his hands out of his pockets in order to defend himself with his small fists, if necessary, against what would now apparently befall him.

The attendant looked at him for a while, then his round, hard gaze became friendly, and he said, "Do you want to come along and help me feed the animals?"

The unexpected kindness and generosity of this offer overwhelmed the little boy completely, and his eyes became bright with unbelieving, fantastic hope.

"Come!" said the animal keeper and reached out his hand, but not all the way to the boy's hand, rather only a short distance in that direction, and the boy had to reach out the rest of the way to meet him. A few seconds passed before suspicion, defiance, fear of being led into a trap, and his own peculiar mocking hatred of any adult cooperation foundered in the hope for unprecedented favor: He was to go into the Dark Continent with the Niger and be permitted to feed his almighty father, the Bengal tiger!

Full of a completely new readiness to yield itself unconditionally, his tightly balled fist finally shoved itself into the animal keeper's powerful, warm hand.

From then on the boy accompanied the attendant almost daily and helped him clean the pens and feed the animals. He proved himself to be clever and quick in comprehending his new activity. When carrying the feed buckets, his thin form demonstrated far more strength and endurance than one would have believed it capable of. He did not seem to know fear at all. He had to be carefully watched to ensure that he did not simply go to the predators in their cages, nor did he hesitate, in spite of his mentor's prohibition, to push the raw meat through the bars to them with his hand, right up to their growlingly raised, reddish lips.

Of course, the animal keeper knew that the animals here in the zoo had already been living in confinement for a long time. They were apathetic; their wild instincts were dulled like a knife with which one has cut bread every day for far too long. He had hardly anything to fear from them. But he was amazed that they did not spit at the new little footman whose smell was still foreign to them and should have aroused their suspicion or long-buried cravings for blood. They seemed to respect him as much as they did their long-time, familiar feeder and keeper.

Of course, the animal keeper knew that the animals here in the zoo had already been living in confinement for a long time. They were apathetic; their wild instincts were dulled like a knife with which one has cut bread every day for far too long. He had hardly anything to fear from them. But he was amazed that they did not spit at the new little footman whose smell was still foreign to them and should have aroused their suspicion or long-buried cravings for blood. They seemed to respect him as much as they did their long-time, familiar feeder and keeper.

It is the secret of fearlessness, thought the attendant.

And then, with a short, sharp feeling of regret and melancholy, he remembered the one second of fear that had put an awful end to his career as an animal tamer years ago.

The doctor had made up his mind to drive out into nature. The day was clear and quiet and thus well suited for passing time leisurely. A little of the unstrained peace that seemed to prevail everywhere in nature where people did not go, would perhaps have a beneficial effect on his nerves. Concealed failure and a vague reduction of self-confidence had been handicapping him inwardly for some time, even though he was disciplined enough to continue his work precisely and conscientiously. The disturbing feeling apparently came from a certain female patient who violently resisted the proven methods, although for inexplicable reasons he took special interest specifically in her. Well, perhaps his personal interest had the effect of reducing his power and increasing her resistance. . .

Suddenly nature seemed not to be the right thing for his frame of mind after all. In the silence of the woods, his thoughts would not find peace, but simply begin all the more to run in the circle of fruitless brooding. He was a man of thought, not of meditation. Resolutely, he parked the car next to the entrance to the zoo and got out. In a dense crowd that strolled easily forward, whose everyday purposeful behavior was calmly relaxed, dissolved in aimless walking along, he too now casually moved, with the feeling of having been released from the ruts of duty. And now for once he wanted to push away any thought of his profession for an hour.

In the blue-green foliage of the chestnuts, the pinkish white, candlelike blossoms stuck out like little, artificially placed wax myrtles, and on the gray ground lay individual, softly rounded petals. Leisurely, the doctor moved with the crowd from cage to cage, watched the animals without particularly looking at them, and read the signs on which the species and also the respective lands of origin were given. Gradually he felt himself released from the uneasiness of that morning.

I can't leave it alone! he thought, suddenly perplexed and amused at himself. Today is one of the rare free days that I can permit myself, and what do I do?! I spend it in front of cells and bars, behind which beings are locked up, in the depths of which the same primeval darknesses slumber as in the souls of my patients in the asylum. Who knows how many of these animals, viewed from the perspective of an animal, have become insane through a forced stay in limited enclosures, which is unnatural according to their instincts?

Yet why should animals have become insane if their freedom was curtailed a little without any cruelty, with good treatment and plenty of food? After all, even human beings had endured their domestication and arrangement in internal and external cages without all that much damage. The enclosure probably caused them some uneasiness, but they were quite happy to live in it. Every human being lived in a cage. Even he himself. He himself even voluntarily.

For he did not even permit himself the healthy and comprehensible disregard that usually led professionally overworked men to take out their pent-up ill humor—which, after all, had to be vented somewhere—on their wives at home. Well, where could you get rid of it otherwise? Who would understand the quite impersonal nature, as it were, of such irritability better than your own wife, who, of course, could place on the other side of the balance innumerable kindnesses and good qualities of her husband that were known only to her and which would outweigh any occasional thoughtlessness?!

Nevertheless, he did not let himself go at home. He did not risk it because he sensed that his nervous irritability was not quite as impersonal as he wanted to believe. For some time it had even been directing itself unmistakably against Melitta, against little things that he had formerly not noticed at all or had even appreciated; for example, her habit of reading the newspaper in his presence as though she had simply forgotten his existence—but she had not forgotten it at all, for she was not given to reading her newspaper quite silently. Rather she habitually threw him a fragment of the reading material now and then, embellished with some personal opinion, and thus tore him away again and again from his own reading material that was much more difficult and demanded much greater concentration. In addition there was her rigidly negative attitude toward anything above or below average, be it in clothing, feelings, matters of personal philosophy of life, politics, or religion. She was reasonable through and through, and because he was just as reasonable, he already knew in advance how she would react to this or that event. She was well formed, middle-sized, pretty but not beautiful; she did everything necessary, never more. She neither saved nor squandered, was not lazy, but did not strive for anything. The only things for which she showed a lively interest were the murder and horror reports in the newspapers. At the same time, she rejected detective novels out of hand "because they are, of course, not true."

He had caught himself thinking that it was strange and symptomatic that murder and rape were entertaining to her, but only if it was a matter of murder that had actually been carried out and rape that had really been committed, because only then did she have the opportunity to become morally indignant. After supper, provided that they did not go to the movies or have guests, she was accustomed to sitting there reading and—following long pauses, always when he had almost forgotten her presence—to sharing her comments with him over the edge of the newspaper, but without looking up.

In principle, one could have no objection to that, he thought, endeavoring as always to do justice to her.

But the intonation, that intonation that was typical for her, drove him crazy, for from it resounded a silent, self-satisfied "Lord, I thank thee, that I am not as they!" be it a matter of excesses in fashion, the suicide attempt of a young person out of love for a ne'er-do-well, the avant-garde mannerisms of modern artists, an unemployed man's act of desperation, or a domestic servant's theft. To say nothing of murderers and sex criminals.

She continually thanks God, in whom she does not believe at all, that of all people she and only she was chosen to be Melitta Klingengast (née Mühlbauer), the wife of Doctor Klingengast, and in so doing she completely overlooks the fact that an average appearance (five foot five and a half while weighing 132 pounds), a tailored suit with a blouse that is always freshly pressed, well-kept hair, and graduation with good marks are not at all the highest purpose of creation and the final aim of all cosmic and earthly situations.

I have been unjust with her the last little while, he inwardly rebuked himself. Didn't I marry her for that very reason? She is normal, quiet, orderly, self-confident; she is good looking and does not allow herself any extravagances. Of course, of course! But, she should not be so terribly convinced of the value of her mediocrity!

And really, why not?

Because—well, for my sake: because I am nervous and get on my own nerves. And because I am just as mediocre as she is. (He actually was likewise five foot five and a half inches tall, while weighing 149 1/2 pounds, but not because he was fat, but only because he had heavier bones.)

The doctor had arrived at the giraffe enclosure and, lost in thought, was staring through the bars at the three large animals that were standing close together at the other end of the fenced-in space, as though they were softly pressing themselves against each other and turning the soft gaze of their small heads this way and that on their long necks. The beautiful design of their spotted hides and the extremely long limbs, combined with the spoonlike ears that grew on short stalks, almost gave the animals the appearance of a bouquet of spotted orchids. They had something decidedly plantlike and soft about them, these gentle monsters of primeval form, full of melancholy grace and defenselessness.

Next to the doctor someone was strewing feed through the bars of the fence. Swaying, one of the animals approached to pick it up while awkwardly spreading its long front legs like fence posts that had been pounded slantingly into the ground, until its mouth could reach the ground. In this position, the giraffe's beauty was distorted into grotesqueness.

At the same time, a boy ran past. He held a walking cane tightly in his hand and let its end rattle across the bars of the fence. It sounded like machine-gun fire.

The giraffe was startled and galloped away, but because the enclosure offered no straight escape path that was suited to its long strides, it had no choice but to run out its long-winded alarm in a circle, and so after hardly twenty strides—strange movements, as though seen through a slow-motion camera—it came past the place where it had been startled, applied the brakes with all four hooves, shrinking back at such an angle that like a swaying tower it threatened to fall over, and continued its flight in a circle without slowing its tempo. It was a soft storming away that rolled along in dilated slowness.

The doctor had no especially pronounced relationship with animals. Of course, he had seen giraffes often enough, in illustrations, in the circus, and in the zoo. But the peculiar gait of the animals, the speed of which stood in continual contradiction to their towerlike bearing and the vegetative charm of their appearance, had never attracted his attention before.

Why—why? Something unknown touched him, a question from primitive times, a not-to-be-clarified, cautioning, silent consternation.

He sought to get hold of the feeling that had fleetingly touched him, by fishing after it with his power of reason, by throwing out concepts and formulations to it like bait, but nothing adhered to them. It was as though, giving in to a lightning-fast, uncontrolled impulse, he had reached into the water to catch a goldfish and were now, uneasily and soaked clear to the top of his clean shirt cuffs, drawing back his empty hand: the fish had slipped away from him. He had only made a fool of himself.

Involuntarily, he looked around in all directions and tugged at his tie. In affirmation of his right to be allowed to remain just as he was, he put on the hat that he had previously held loosely in his hand and strolled on with measured strides.

Just what did the giraffe matter to him?! Without being deprived of even the slightest thing, one could live for sixty years without knowing the fact that somewhere else there were giraffes, dappled, exotic fruits on long, wavering stems, which suddenly became alarmed and began to run.

After all, he was neither a hunting lion nor an animal keeper. Rather, he was Dr. Karl Klingengast, director of two scientific organizations, physician in the renowned Rose Hill Clinic, married, Catholic, Austrian citizen, forty years old, five foot five and a half tall. Thank God...

... that I am not like them! Who them? What them? The giraffes perhaps? he thought in confusion.

And then these thoughts followed the logic of that thinking in random jumps: It is completely possible that it is only my great similarity to Melitta that arouses me against her that way. You cannot continually look into a mirror. But he bluntly pushed the thought away: Nonsense! Would I perhaps like my wife to have a spotted neck and spoonlike ears that rotate on stalks? Unfortunately, it is difficult and requires many detours to return in random leaps of thought to the place from which you began.

Then external events released him from his brooding. He was just approaching a cluster of people who were agitatedly pressing around a focal point, and when he had arrived, he saw a man with an attendant's kepi and a badge on the lapel of his jacket carrying a boy in his arms through the crowd, a boy, however, who was already past the age at which children have to be carried.

His senses were trained to make his brain immediately and clearly aware of everything that could perhaps make his medical assistance necessary.

"What has happened here?" he asked, joining the others.

"The little boy jumped from the barrier and hurt himself," someone said.

Klingengast pressed his way through and took off his hat before the attendant.

"I am a physician."

The boy was pale, but he did not utter a sound of pain. Rather, his slanted, yellowish eyes stared darkly and disapprovingly at the sympathetic spectators and the doctor.

"It probably isn't too bad," said the attendant. "But would you please come along and look at his ankle?"

The three of them entered the attendant's apartment. The boy was placed on the bed and immediately attempted to resist the doctor by kicking when the latter reached for his foot.

"Now, now, just be calm," said Klingengast. "It will soon be over."

He set the sprained ankle back in joint.

"Good!" he then said appreciatively. "He didn't even cry out. Does it still hurt?"

The boy snorted audibly and scornfully through his nose and remained silent. The doctor began bandaging the ankle with a strip of gauze from the attendant's first aid kit.

"Is he your boy?" he asked the attendant.

"No. I have no idea at all where he belongs. He sometimes helps me with the animals."

"Well, what is your name?" The doctor now turned to the little boy.

"Josef."

"Just Josef? Or do you perhaps have another name?"

It was supposed to sound playfully ironic, but he hardly ever hit the right tone, neither with children nor with that particular kind of patients who. . .

The boy blinked scornfully at him. With a meaningful nod from the doctor to the attendant he said, including the latter in an insolent collusion, "That's what he thinks!" But the attendant was not disposed to let that sort of thing pass. His gaze put the little boy in his place, and he finally condescended to answer.

"My name is Josef Kutian."

"Kutian. You say, Kutian? And where do you live?" Klingengast regarded the boy attentively and seemed to be thinking about something.

"In Lainz. On the other side of the railroad crossing. Our street doesn't have a name any more, because it has been torn down, except for our house."

"Is that the district between the railroad tracks and the old folks' home?"

"Yes, there."

"But that's pretty far from here."

"Not far at all!"

"It will be better if the boy doesn't overtax his foot now," the doctor said to the attendant. "I'll take him home in my car. Perhaps it would be possible for me to drive in this far to pick up the patient?"

"Certainly," the attendant answered. "If you would really be so kind? I'd be grateful to you for that. I feel somewhat responsible for the boy. Well, Josef, how about that? Now you can ride in the car! I'll call the gatekeeper at the main gate and notify him so that he'll let you drive in."

Having grown completely silent and docile with excitement at the prospect of this unprecedented adventure, the boy let himself be lifted into the car. He had already forgotten the aching ankle.

In the car the distance was certainly not far. The boy was otherwise used to completing it in a loose trot without stopping. When they passed the railroad crossing, on the right side an entire district of new, tall municipal buildings appeared, with stretches of green between them, but to the left, before the tract began that had already been laid out for new construction, a pavilionlike form still stood, in which there was a dairy store, and next to it a low ramshackle building with crooked walls.

"There it is," said the boy and pointed to the dilapidated house with the large patches of fungus on the grayish-yellow plasterwork and narrow, deeply hollowed window holes that gaped from the moldy walls like sunken eyes. The broad wooden door with the old sun symbol led inside without stair or step, into a cool, plastered passageway that, because of its lightlessness, had something cavelike about it and brewed in an indescribable vapor of garbage, dampness, cooking smell, and fresh earth. On the right side, the boy pounded hard with his fist against an iron door that was ajar. It yielded quiveringly beneath the blows and opened toward the inside, leading into a pitch black chamber of no more than two meters square; and from this anteroom they went through a wooden door into the narrow kitchen that received enough light from one of the dormer windows to expose its wretchedness without mercy. The doctor registered briefly an old tiled stove with an open chimney, a stand with a dirty red-flowered curtain, a mud-crusted man's shoe that lay in the middle of the room on the brick floor like a damaged boat, many empty bottles and indefinable household junk that looked as if it had been gathered up from rubbish heaps and provisionally repaired.

A doorless opening led into the next room. The boy limped inside, and the physician followed him and peered somewhat disgustedly into what probably represented a family's bedroom: a damp square room with three primitive bedsteads, a chair, a table, and a wardrobe, the door of which yawned open because it had only three legs and leaned dangerously to one side.

From one of the bedsteads a man straightened up and growled in a hoarse voice, "What's going on?"

"I hurt myself!" said the boy in a tone of defiant self-defense and raised his bandaged foot as proof.

"Little devil!" the man bawled, bent with an effort under the bed, and the second dirty shoe suddenly whistled past the boy—who quickly ducked—and slammed against the wall.

"Listen, your son. . . ," the doctor began.

But the apparently drunken man interrupted him: "Son, son! He is not mine anyhow. . ." The rest died in mumbling and yawning groans and then suddenly changed to soft snoring. The boy did not seem at all intimidated by his father's anger. Tranquilly he limped up to the bed, suddenly bent forward from a barely safe distance, punched the sleeping man hard in the ribs, and screamed, "Where's Grandmother? Father, can't you hear? I want to know where Grandmother is!"

The man came to himself and struck angrily toward the side where the boy stood, but the boy calmly moved out of his way. Then the man murmured, "In the garden. How should I know?" With that he fell asleep again.

The boy climbed up on the chair that stood beneath the back wall's dormer window and peered out through the bars.

"Grandmother!" he yelled, and after a while again, "Grandmother!" But his yelling was only intended to be theoretical. He apparently expected no answer, for he knew that it could not come. "She's hard of hearing," he said, explaining the ceremony to the guest. And then he called once more, half to prove it, half not to have omitted anything, "Grandmother!"

Then he climbed down from the chair and again led the physician through the narrow kitchen, the dark anteroom, and the paved passageway, this time, however, out the back way into the yard. And here poverty, filth, and the hopelessness of urban squalor suddenly lost all horror, and the house gate's sun symbol had not deceived after all.

For behind the house whose roof ridge suggested the back of a broken-down mare with its protruding ridge beams and rafters between which the silvery shingle roof had sunken in like a creased horse hide, there was a strip of ground with some heads of cabbage, tomato plants along the sunny wall, green heads of lettuce, and on the rise of the former hotbed even pumpkins flourished. In the middle of the garden a faded bundle of old clothing was bent over close to the ground, and two brown, rough hands pulled the weeds.

Now she straightened up and looked toward the window. Her face was rawboned and broad, very broad. It rested like a moss-covered boulder on the plinth of her still erect, broad shoulders. But she was nevertheless old and worn out. Her breasts lay deformed like two half-full bags on the protruding curvature of her body. Thus for seconds she stood still, a monument of petrified indifference. Her eyes looked at the doctor who came with the boy through the garden from the entrance, without amazement, nervousness, or curiosity. They were gray. But in their expression they resembled the boy's eyes. Their silent scorn, the irony of the individual who has nothing more to lose and therefore also nothing more to fear, this scorn was the old and venerable, petrified form of the same scorn that could glitter in the boy's golden eyes, even before defiance and hate.

"Grandmother, I hurt myself!" the boy called triumphantly, and again he lifted the proof, the bandaged foot.

"The little boy sprained his foot," the doctor added. Silently she wiped her hands off in her apron and pulled the crooked kerchief further down on her forehead.

"He should lie quietly and receive compresses made with basic aluminum acetate."

"So!" she said, sullenly deprecating.

She took a large, clumsy step out over the cabbage bed and onto the hardened path that was hardly a foot wide, untied her apron, shook it out, and tied it on again.

"By the way, it's not the little boy's fault," Klingengast hastily said in order to save his protege from additional blows or from objects flying through the air.

The old woman turned her face toward the boy. Her glance seemed to say: He? It's always his fault.

"Is your father awake?" she asked him, but without anger, resigned, as you perhaps thoughtlessly ask if it is raining while the first fat drops are already hitting you in the face.

How peculiar they are, Klingengast thought. They do and say everything as if they knew that it is quite senseless anyway, but they seem to have the feeling that they must do and say something nevertheless, if they are alive.

"He's asleep," said the boy and made illustrative snoring sounds.

"The gentleman says you should lie down."

"The gentleman is a doctor!" shrieked the boy and suddenly sprang toward her, wildly gesticulating and making loud snoring noises, as if he intended to hit her. "I rode in a car! So there!"

Mechanically she lifted her right hand to hit him, but thought better of it, especially since the boy was already out of reach again.

"Go inside and lie down by your father. But don't wake him up."

Strangely enough, the boy obeyed immediately. After the hysterical jumping around, his foot was probably hurting again, or perhaps he no longer had any desire to be with the doctor and his grandmother. Without farewell and limping badly, he disappeared into the house.

The physician sat down on the narrow bench that leaned against the back wall of the house resting on two poles that were already rotten next to the ground. Slowly the old woman shuffled closer and sat down next to him.

"Basic aluminum acetate," he repeated and clung to the specialized knowledge that gave him superiority, for a peculiar and completely unfounded uncertainty had gripped him. "I'll write it down for you here. You can obtain it in any pharmacy." And when she remained silent: "Make compresses and keep him as quiet as possible for a few days."

"Him and keeping quiet!" she finally said and put the slip of paper in her apron pocket. Then she was silent again.

It was, in fact, so very quiet behind the house, almost as still as in the country, in the middle of the densely populated suburban housing development with enormous apartment blocks, buses, and cafes. Then a sound pressed its way into this island of silence. From very far away the horn of an ambulance sounded, but the hectic sound died away in the garden, as though here nothing were taken very seriously, not even the fact that anyone could be stricken by illness sometime and be brought to the nearby nursing home to die. The wind lifted a few loose threads of bark and hesitatingly let them fall again. In the hotbed, a yellow pumpkin blossom glowed like a star amid the bristly, tangled foliage of the creeping vines. The spot of cultivated earth was edged with a row of red and yellow peasant flowers, pansies and primroses and crocuses that stood out brightly in front of the three-story fire wall of the next house. The old woman sat motionless, silent, and rigid next to him. It was strange that this stone block of old age and joyless existence had planted flowers!

He would have liked to ask her a few things, but he was intimidated by her inhospitable silence on the piece of ground that she owned and had cultivated.

Suddenly she turned her head to face him. She looked at him. Her mouth, which had become thin and sullen, even twisted into a slight, cunning, toothless smile, as though she knew something that he could have absolutely no idea about. Confused, he smiled back. Then he stood up and took off his hat in a gesture of farewell.

"So, make compresses!" he repeated disconcertedly. "It's not as bad as it looks."

"Do you think so?" It sounded enigmatically crafty, wry. But then she added almost good-naturedly, "Everything always straightens itself out, Doctor."

Peculiar person, he thought. Rather devious. And the little boy, he is not quite normal either.

The grandmother remained sitting on the bench. Thoughtfully she plucked the individual brown stems from her dress, dried fragments of the kind that usually cling when you brush against dry bushes in passing. Her face relaxed a little as she sat so idly in the late afternoon sun. It was a yellow-brown face with wrinkles as fine and close together as cobwebs. The wrinkles, however, could take nothing from its strong, lean structure. It was the simple face of an old peasant woman for whom births and deaths, hail and sunshine, happiness and unhappiness had long ago melted together into a mystical unity.

She came from the country, from one of those small villages in Burgenland that consist of a dusty country road next to ponds and a gutter, two rows of white houses that are connected to each other by flying buttress gates and have their narrow ends facing the street, and a line of white, fatted geese leisurely waddling down the middle of the road. For the old woman, the image of such a village was still what she would call home, although she had not been there for about fifty years.

She had come to Vienna at the age of fourteen and had started work as a servant girl. In those days that young fellow, the doctor, was not even alive yet, she thought. She giggled scornfully, as though the circumstance that she was so much older and had so much more life behind her gave her a secret superiority over him.

Anna had served her employers for fifteen years and had saved her pennies. After those fifteen years, she still wore her peasant dresses, petticoats, boots and aprons, a bandanna, and in the winter her own mother's large, black, woolen shawl. She had never owned a coat in her life.

She was a rather large girl with a thick pigtail, red lips, and white teeth that glowed from the yellowish-brown face. In her twentieth year she became engaged to a young worker whom she immediately presented to her mistress. He then received permission to drink coffee with her in the kitchen on Sunday afternoons. On her day off they went to the Prater or for a walk on Bald Hill, and while doing so they sometimes kissed. He did not receive more; in those days it was still not generally customary that a man received more before the wedding, and she felt no regret about that. She had accepted him without great passion because he was a sober, decent person, and after all, she had to marry somebody sometime.

So she became twenty-five and thirty years old.

The few scenes from the past arose like colored pictures from a peep-show. They had given her life all of its decisive stimuli.

First the market. She stood there in her bandanna and apron, the handle of the filled basket over her arm, between the stands full of plucked chickens and the boxes with eggs on excelsior, green piles of lettuce, and wooden baskets full of apricots, red apples, and plums. And suddenly she was overcome by a feeling like she had at home when she looked up from the turnip field and the long white road glittered and sparkled in the sun, until she suddenly became oddly aware of herself: she knelt there, next to that road, motionless as a stone, and the road ran on and on, hopping and dancing over insignificant rises, ever onward out into infinity.

The same feeling overcame her now at the market: She stood there as though she had fallen asleep a hundred years ago while standing, and only the colored apples and the pale green heads of cabbage grew and changed. Things blossomed, ripened, and wilted around her, and she alone still stood there just as motionless...

She was "stalled like a tram," her mistress often reproachfully said.

She stood in the others' way, and it was unavoidable that in the bustle of the market someone finally bumped against her basket, and the red apple that had lain on top rolled onto the pavement. While she clumsily bent after it after waking with a start from her dream-glutted condition, the cabbage heads also rolled out of her basket, and a few pink onions hopped after them.

Confused, she placed the half-empty shopping basket on the ground, crouched down, and reached for the vegetables between the legs of the inattentive people who were pressing by. She failed only to reach the red apple. It had rolled on in front of two enormously elegant, bright yellow, pointed men's shoes that had almost stumbled over it.

"Jeez!" she murmured, moving along on her knees, a bit behind the apple. Then a head of black hair, glistening with pomade and parted in an unbelievably straight, cream-white line, bent down into her field of view, and a long-fingered man's hand with a gold signet ring on its index finger reached for the apple, picked it up, and it was gone! But just as unexpectedly, the red apple suddenly dropped from above into her basket, which was still standing next to her on the pavement, and a voice, as pomade-smooth and silky soft as the black hair had been earlier, pressed into her ears.

She did not understand what the voice said. Looking up, she saw a thick black moustache like the ones that the young men back home wore, and that encouraged her a little, even though the speaker was otherwise a distinguished man, from his yellow shoes to the white part line. She stared at him admiringly and in total confusion, and hardly brought forth a word of thanks.

"Stand up, my pretty child," the gentleman said amiably.

Hastily and deeply ashamed, she got up from her knees. With the gloves that he held loosely in his left hand, he brushed the dust from her apron, and in the process, as if by magic, two more red-cheeked apples fell from the broad hem of her skirt into the basket.

Astonished, she slapped her cheek and neck with her left hand, a movement that usually expressed her fright or amazement, while her mouth remained open and speechless; for the path from experience to the spoken word was long and rugged, and she was actually not so much a dreamer as a person of extremely slow reaction ability, and was therefore never able to find that path quickly enough, so that the abbreviation of speechless gesture was all that she had left.

Still mute and red in the face, with her eyes and their thick blond lashes deeply lowered, she then trotted along next to the yellow oxfords, while to her most painful embarrassment the distinguished gentleman carried the basket and spoke in a steady stream. And before she had regained her composure enough to say something herself, she was already standing in front of the villa on Hunting Lodge Lane with the basket in one hand and a complimentary ticket for the evening circus performance in the other. And the gentleman with the moustache was bobbing elegantly and light-footedly out of sight around the corner.

She was always standing or kneeling motionless as a stone somewhere. And life skipped flickeringly past her round gaze and the mouth that stood open in speechless amazement. At least, that is how it had been as long as she was young, and she had been young right up until a very specific day—afterward her youth was gone overnight—young and foolish and as amazed as a goose that one grabs beneath the wings to carry it away to slaughter.

She could now no longer exactly remember what followed then. It had probably already become blurred at the time, in the steam and smoke of his magic tricks and in the mist of a happiness that the old woman could now no longer comprehend, but rather shook her head at seeing it in the young people of the time: Love. Love? Silly ninnies!

But one image was sharply engraved in her memory and now still held for her more reality than her seduction to a warm and shimmering happiness that had long ago become outdated.

It was the sink in the beautiful, bright kitchen in the house where she had served, with the golden brass faucet that she had tenderly cleaned with metal polish every Saturday for fifteen years. For water that always flowed, conjured forth with a flick of the wrist, and which dried up in response to a similar flick of the wrist, was one of the great miracles of city life for someone who had already been dragging heavy buckets home from the village spring at the age of seven, when cold splashes of water had sloshed into her wooden clogs because the burden had caused her to lean and sway. Hot and cold water without effort, metal polish and soap flakes, clean dishes and glistening brass, those were things that filled her life with beauty and joy. She considered washing dishes to be an agreeably unhurried afternoon pursuit, no different than when her mistress enjoyed knitting cobweb-fine doilies in her leisure time.

But on the day in question, as she bent over the silently steaming wash water and saw the vegetable fragments floating on top of it, and as the greasy vapor rose into her nose, her stomach suddenly heaved, and she immediately knew what was wrong with her. Such a thing was a disgrace, to be sure, but still a disgrace that occurred frequently without one having to die of it.

When her fiancé came in the evening, her eyes were red from crying. He had already been suspicious for several weeks because she had had little time for him and had nothing at all to say anymore when they were together. Now it was not difficult for him to wrest a confession from her. Then he reviled her, after that he began to cry, and finally he made demands of her. But she had awakened so suddenly from her "stalled-tram" condition, that without any experience in things of that sort she knew: If I give in, I will get him to marry me. Suddenly, however, it made her angry that a man who was no seducer at all and had attempted nothing before, now, in her embarrassing situation, wanted to seduce her. Without clearly knowing why, she loathed the carrion-eater that followed the predator to gnaw at the remains. Her rejection made him so angry that he forgot himself and began to scream at her, and through that they attracted the attention of her mistress, and everything came out. But it would have come out sooner or later anyway.

She was dismissed with a week's notice.

First she tried to reach the magician, but he did not have time to listen to her. His performance was about to begin, and of course she was not able to formulate a sentence in three minutes and get it out of her mouth. He did not come to the rendezvous that he agreed upon for the next day in order to get rid of her. Then she realized that she had to take care of herself. The next morning she left the house before her week was up and departed with her belongings and savings book, determined to plunge immediately into the desperate, irreversible situation. She felt powers grow within her that sufficed to make everything possible that was necessary.

There was no point in looking for a new position; in a few months they would be able to tell by looking at her and throw her out again. She wandered out onto the windy hill beyond the last houses of that part of town and sat down there in the grass where she could look down on the enormous tapered tent of the circus.

She deliberated, and that lasted a long time, for it was an occupation to which in the fullness and security of life she had never before had to submit herself.

The old booth owner came out of the wooden hut in which she sold sweets and refreshments all summer and began to talk with her. As long as the circus remained there, she kept her business open until late at night, for after the performance she could still count on customers. Even Anna with her magician had climbed up here once or twice. First they had drunk a bottle of beer at the old woman's place, then they had wandered deeper into the bushes. Today she was there alone for the first time. The old woman knew what to make of that, and of course the bundle with Anna's belongings spoke in no uncertain terms.

An hour later, Anna's immediate future had been well and reasonably decided. The old woman had a little house; there Anna moved into the damp cubicle with the closet whose door already hung slanted open in those days. From then on she was to manage the stand, for the old woman already felt too weak to run the business alone. For as long as she lived, Anna was to care for her; after that, the house and the business would be bequeathed to her.

It was a kind of annuity from which both could profit.

Late in the evening she put on a fresh scarf and went to the circus again to inform the magician. She herself did not believe that he would marry her—such an elegant man and a magician besides! Actually, she did not understand how she had arrived at all at the honor of having been led into disgrace by him. Presumably, the trace of dialect color that remained in his language had brought them together. It was the same dialect that Anna spoke in its unadulterated form. Perhaps it was the faded memory of a village with two rows of white houses and a line of waddling geese along the brook, and of a woman in coarse knee boots, with fustian petticoats and a broad, brown face that glowed in the sun, who had been his mother in that village, which, like Anna's village, lay in Burgenland. Perhaps it would impress him if he learned how much she had saved and that a roof and bed and a basic livelihood were already provided. He would probably not marry her in spite of that, but then not deny that he was the father, so that she would not have to stand there as somebody who did not even know who her child's father was.

A person learns to calculate so quickly; the path from dream into reality is so short: a catwalk across the abyss of misery.

Her boots stumbled ponderously across the circus ground that had been trampled by many feet, but—her broad hand flew up with a start, and she slapped her cheek—the great tent had disappeared. In the glow of torches and fires the colorful wagons stood around ready to leave, people yelled commands at each other, ropes were being coiled up, lights and shadows hastened across stakes, tarpaulins, and cages.

She had halfway expected something like that. A circus cannot remain in the same city forever. She felt her way forward between unrecognizable colossi and bizarre objects, stumbled over an iron chain that was stretched tight to a stake before her feet, almost rammed a wagon tongue into her body, reached around for something to hold on to, and caught hold of a couple of angular iron bars. Suddenly, two green eyes glowed close in front of her, stinking breath surged toward her, and a hissing rumble arose and increased to an angry roar. She let go of the bars, as though they were glowing hot, and, mute with horror, slapped her cheek and neck with the flat of her hand. Then for a few seconds she saw black, her heart faltered, and she almost fainted.

But then the magician appeared next to her and lifted a lantern to see who was doing something around the predator cages that had already been loaded on the carriages. Snarling, the Bengal tiger withdrew to the back wall of the cage. His fur glowed wonderfully black and gold in the lantern light, and the white fangs gleamed dangerously. His shadow brushed jaggedly up the iron bars. For a few moments the world seemed to be an infinitely black prison full of fear, across which the tiger stripes danced along, royally and cruelly, like the golden lashes of a whip.

Anna felt a peculiar tugging in the hollows of her knees, but it did not come from fright alone, because mixed with her horror was a sucking, sweet weakness, an incomprehensible desire that changed to dizziness and drew her into a swirling vortex. She sank onto a pile of canvas and remained lying there, half crouching, incapable of tearing her eyes away from the horrible, green gaze of the tiger.

And once again, this time experienced to the utmost extreme, it was that moment of self-alienation that was already remotely familiar to her. Heavy and motionless, she lay there, a field stone sunk halfway into the earth, with her stonily immovable soul and a heart like stone, full of heaviness and emptiness, while the earth continued to revolve around her.

His assurance, that the tiger was in the cage, of course, and could do nothing to her, rushed past her ears, unheard and not understood. The soft voice finally became cold and impatient. That finally brought her to herself, and she remembered her life, her condition, the reason for her coming, but only like the fate of someone else that she had indifferently read somewhere. It was perhaps for that reason that her words had no effect at all. She was not pleading for herself but for a certain Anna whom she had once known. He promised to come again soon, and then they would look to the future.

She did not believe a word he said, but it had become strangely unimportant to her. She was alone with her destiny, far away from him. Later it often seemed to her as though something from the tiger had rubbed off on her, and in the following years that gave her strength to defend herself. First you learn to think, then you learn to scratch. The meekness, the quiet, broad, motionlessly kneeling, rurally eastern, servant-girl humility of her youth was as if it had been blown away, and it never returned to her.

With a frugal sense of justice, she cared for the old woman in whose house she now lived, but even while the woman was still alive, Anna was able to do her out of the house, the business license, and the collapsible sales booth. She also inconsiderately saddled her with the child that she brought into the world, little Mitzi, when she herself did not have time. She quarreled with the old woman, remaining coldly and cleverly under control, defrauded or fed her, depending upon her mood. It was one of those relationships full of trifling quarrels and hate, full of necessarily feigned kindnesses and unavoidable sacrifices, where the roles of the stronger and the underdog are unceasingly exchanged and the position of the current victor is used to take revenge for occasional defeats through little humiliations and acts of spite. For misery does not always teach to pray, but sometimes also to kick.

One day about five years later, from her elevated seat in the wooden booth, peering out between a pickle jar, the covered cheese dish, and a few fly-specked tin cans full of cotton candy, Anna saw a long procession of colorfully painted circus wagons approach and stop on the large meadow at the foot of the hill.

Mitzi was a beautiful child with her father's fine facial features and his long limbs—for a five-year-old, she was extraordinarily tall and slender—and in addition she had inherited her mother's thick, curly hair and rosy lips. Anna knew what she wanted, when, on a weekday, she put a freshly starched dress and the white Sunday stockings on the little girl and unraveled her braids so that her hair could wind around her lovely face like a glistening, curly mane. In her boots and petticoats, she took the child by the hand and walked next to Mitzi looking like the peasant governess of a spoiled little angel.

The magician recognized her immediately.

"Well what do you want this time?" he asked irritatedly, but also uncertainly, because he himself realized that after a waiting period of five years he had no right to say: "this time."

But Anna was curt with him, and her voice let no doubt arise about the absolute indifference of her feelings.

"I? Nothing." A short, contemptuous pause. "This girl here just wants to become acquainted with her father." With that she resolutely pushed the child toward him.

"My, but she's pretty!" he said dumbfoundedly.

Anna nodded in agreement, as if she had always claimed that very thing and was now about to prove it to him. And Mitzi did what had been drummed into her head at home. She took a step toward the strange man, curtsied politely, looked at him with her sweetest child's gaze, and said, "Greetings, dear Father!" The old-fashioned, deferential phrasing and the child's beauty had their effect. When the circus moved on a few weeks later, he took Mitzi with him. Her father had decided to give her a higher education and to make a child prodigy out of her. There followed a life full of hard physical work, with blows now and then, but no more than she had also received from her mother at home. Under the strict training, her joints became soft and limber, and she fearlessly tried the tightrope and working with horses, the same way that she tried dancing. But alas, the body was willing, but the spirit too weak, even for a profession based upon the body's ability. She simply lacked presence of mind. She had inherited her mother's slow, stonily benumbed perceptive faculty, and what happened to the giant species of animals that died out because their heads were too far from their extremities, also happened to her. Before she comprehended that a balancing movement was necessary, she fell into the net; before she recognized that a colored hoop or a ball came flying at her, they were already rolling in the sand. Her father, the magician, called this trait: "slow-witted."

At the age of eight, when she had already outgrown the role of a golden-haired elf whose contrastingly charming beauty and grace had helped a coarse clown act to achieve success with the public, her father lost all interest in her and sent her home again, provided with some money, so that she could attend school.

Nor did school bring her the joys and successes of normal children, any more than the circus had been able to give her the glistening, laboriously achieved triumphs of nonbourgeois creatures. Because the other girl pupils were one or two years younger than she was, the size of her body was twice as noticeable and brought her a lot of teasing. She stood around among the others as lonely as a poplar tree on a meadow. Clever, urban, sharp-tongued ridicule, for the complete understanding of which she lacked the intelligence, but which she nevertheless painfully suspected, surged around her tall hips day after day, while the poor, dumb head never really mastered the subject matter and in its sad loftiness soon assumed an expression of amazement and injury that never left it for the rest of her life. Only in her physical education class—which at the time, however, was among the least important subsidiary subjects—was she able to win the admiration of the other children through her acrobatic nimbleness. For that reason, she voluntarily continued to train at home in order not to lose as well the only sign of favoritism that fate had given her.

When she was not yet twelve, she was already beginning to let her wondering, sad gaze wander down to her imposingly formed mother. Hard work had made Anna broader and at the same time shorter; her body gave the impression of being compressed into the form of an enormous box, but she was still a tall woman.

The old woman from whom she had taken over the house and business had died; everything legally belonged to Anna, and she felt comparatively wealthy. But it was now the time of the economic depression, and the many unemployed people who camped on the hill with bread and lard and a bottle of malt coffee, with playing cards and mending kits, while their children flew homemade kites, played with balls of rags, or fought, could only seldom buy fifty grams of sour candy or a roll with sausage and a bottle of beer. The tall Mitzi's insatiable appetite began to pursue her mother right into her dreams. So one day, with the assistance of the pensioner who had his allotment garden on the slope of the hill, she wrote a letter that followed the circus from city to city for almost a year before it finally reached the magician's hands. In that letter she reported that Mitzi had become tall and very pretty and asked if he could now use her in the circus.

Therefore, soon after that Mitzi returned to the circus after all. A few years later, under the sonorous name of "Mona Belinda," she appeared in an act with her father, specifically as a virgin who was sawed in two. In every performance, she was placed in a box in her spangled tricot, sawed in half, and restored again through black magic.

The wind was always blowing across the top of the hill with the clear view of the large meadow, allotment gardens, garbage dumps, and little project houses on the left, and the giant complexes of new municipal buildings on the right, and behind them, as a border toward the horizon, the woody ridge of the Lainz Animal Refuge. It was not a sharp wind, nor a zephyr of a lyrical nature, but the bracing, cheerful, strong wind of the suburbs, the wind for the barefoot children who chased the kites, who were always hungry and always dirty. It was also this wind that prematurely covered Anna's cheeks with innumerable thin, black lines and dried out her skin, tanning it a deeper brown, as if she were already to be transformed into a mummy while she was still alive. By the way, that is how they all looked, those who lay here for days in the grass, played cards, and waited for better times, senselessly passing the time in the involuntary freedom of their unemployment. But the freedom of the unemployed is only an invisible cage. In it they lounged around on the windy grass knoll that had to take the place of nature and authentic human reality for them, on old overcoats, with bread and a bottle of coffee next to them, while their strength tugged at the facts to which they were tethered and wanted to break out into something useful; until the will gradually wore out and stolidly lay down next to the shabby, resting figure, no differently than if the wind had blown a rain-soaked, crumpled scrap of paper next to it. And then the will gradually lost its muscles, just as the muscles on their inactive arms also dwindled away.

They did not look much different than Anna: prematurely withered, colorless; somewhat more haggard in their urban than she in her rural poverty; just as hard-bitten, sly, and determined not to starve, but not as stoic, immovable as she was. There was sometimes underground rumbling; grumbling rang out everywhere where they stood together in groups. These revolutionaries who resisted as if they did not believe in the unavoidable were usually newcomers to the freedom of the unemployed. In them life still expressed itself powerfully and plainly as anger and as the hope that is contained in anger. But wisdom holds out to life its unrelenting "What for?" It says that it is better to live as little as possible. He who does not tug at the chain is not tethered. He can starve in peace. Can't he be quiet for this short time? Only as long as life lasts. It is soon gone as though it had never been.

The young unskilled laborer Josef Kutian was not among those who were inclined to obtain by force their right to another existence that was more worthy of a human being. The big "What for?" had taken him on its soft and weary wings. He glided along that way. The degree of his hopelessness had almost reached the bounds of wisdom, those bounds at which Anna stood motionless like a moss-covered landmark that separates the fields of living anger from that fallow land of hardened patience with a few scornful thistles on it.

On the day when Kutian became ineligible for benefits and could no longer even expect to receive unemployment compensation, he drank away the last of his money at Anna's sales booth. It was fine with her as long as he immediately paid for each bottle before he carried it to the wooden table at the edge of the bushes. She did not even give him credit for the deposit on the first bottle, although she could easily keep her eye on him from the booth as he sat there with his arms propped up and his head hanging down. When he had nothing more to spend for drink, but his intoxication was not yet sufficient to let him forget his misery, he asked her if she would give him a bottle of beer on credit.

"No," said Anna curtly. "Nobody gets credit."

He stared at her from gloomy eyes, but he bridled his vague longing to smash her hut to pieces. She watched him carefully and recognized that he was good-natured.

"You can help me take down the stand this evening," she said. "I'm going to close down for this year. It's already too cold."

He nodded his agreement and received a roll with sausage and a bottle of beer as an advance payment for the work. Then he slept on the bench in the cool October wind until evening.

Anna went over now and then and looked at his face, as though she were trying to decipher a difficult text, the text of a contract in which one might suspect traps and unexpected deceptions. It was a coarse but not an evil face. She looked searchingly at the body that belonged to it. The legs were very short and crooked, but extraordinarily sturdy; the shoulders were broad, and the head sat very tightly on them. Those with thin necks and large Adam's apples were vultures; those with long soft necks were geese; those with thick necks were good draft oxen. She examined his arms the way you evaluate the worth of an animal at a cattle market. They were lean, but the joints were bony and knotty and sinewy.

She went back behind the sales counter and calculated with the help of her fingers, using the fingers of her left hand for the bad that could always be expected, the fingers of her right hand for the scant profit that could possibly be gained from all of the bad.

During the summer, the income from the stand barely sufficed to live on; in the winter Mitzi regularly sent her mother some money. Sometimes the magician enclosed a banknote for firewood. All of that was not enough for two. But behind the house vegetables could be planted; you could obtain permits to pick up deadwood, gather berries and mushrooms, and carry them to market; you could steal Christmas trees before Christmas and sell flowers in the spring.

You could not accomplish all that very well alone, and not at all if you had to take care of a business. She finally came to the conclusion that it would not be so bad to have a man in the house.

In the evening she awakened Kutian, and while they were taking down the stand she told him the results of her calculations piece by piece. She set two conditions: that he did not drink and that he left her alone, for she "was no longer curious." He agreed. For him it meant social advancement, that he no longer had to sleep in the shelter but was permitted to sleep in the damp room, that she cooked for him and mended his clothing. He was sincerely thankful to her and proved himself willing and resourceful in tracking down new small sources of income. He also drank little; he was actually no drunkard as soon as he had no serious reason to long for release in unconsciousness. . .

Now the sun had gone down behind the slanting roof ridge; occasionally, watery, yellow bundles of light still flashed up around the chimney like the spray of a jet of water that is too sharp against the railing of the spring when you lift away the full bucket. The wall of the house and the vegetable garden lay in the shadows. Ashes seemed to fall across the bright colors.

Old Anna lifted herself from the bench and went into the house. In the entrance, she turned around once more out of habit and looked to see if she had forgotten anything, a rake or the cultivator.

The pumpkin blossom had folded shut for the night.

A dislocated foot or a life out of joint, everything rights itself, she felt. Life—life indeed... It became upset and flickered and changed full of officiousness; it passed by like a circus; everything passed by that way, colorful wagons, beet fields, kites in the September wind, unemployment and employment again, full beer bottles and empty beer bottles... She stood like a stone, empty and heavy, and very far away from happiness and pain and the whole circus.

Again the ambulance blew its siren in the distance. It stopped in front of the home for the aged at the end of the street. A litter was pushed from the white-painted box with the red cross on it. Something was tied down on it, but it was something so shabby and thin, already nothing really physical at all. Only the eyes, clouded by great weariness, full of animal fear and human resignation, showed how much feeling was still alive in this shriveled bundle of refuse from nature's great material warehouse.

Our turn will also come, thought Anna. Everyone's turn comes. And it appeased her like her own most personal secret revenge: as if only because old Anna assentingly and noddingly accepted the necessity of dying, the death of all others, of the poor as well as the rich, of the suffering and the happy, was ensured.

The grandmother, as Kutian already familiarly called Anna, was not at home at the time. She was on her way with her flower basket from cafe to cafe. It was spring.

When someone knocked, Kutian opened the door. Outside stood an unfamiliar lady.

Mitzi had to bend down when she entered the kitchen, and then she straightened up, and Kutian had to look up at her. He stood speechless in front of her. He had not seen anything like it before: that fabulous height, the silky hair that was nothing but stiff, round curls, the soft, powdered skin, and the dress, more colorful and cut lower than what he was accustomed to seeing in his surroundings. To him it was as though a supernatural being had entered the wretched kitchen, and everything around paled to misery-gray shabbiness.

Her cheek exhibited a large red mark that ran down over her throat into the low-necked dress and disappeared as a slender fiery serpent between her high breasts. His glance involuntarily followed this serpent's small, deft twists again and again, as far as they could be seen, only to turn away then in confusion, for insolence or indecent staring was not Kutian's way at all. He had not previously lived carefree enough to be able to look around for women very much.

When a man has never received more than the meager, gray necessities, and fate suddenly offers him something so completely unnecessary and impractical: a woman who is two meters tall, much more woman than one needs for life and love, unusual beauty and two meters of it all at once, beyond that a scar that no other woman has, a unique medal of fate whose origin and meaning seem unexplainable—must such a man then not lose his head, a man who has only laboriously learned to add up advantages but cannot comprehend the multiplication of beauty and the squaring and cubing of excess?

She was the first woman from whom he could not turn away his eyes; she astounded him immeasurably. There were only two ways of looking at this female phenomenon: the respectfully inhibited glance upward at her, and after that, as though hypnotized, letting the eyes wander gropingly downward along the red scar to her breasts; and, when she turned her back to him, his glances pressed in the opposite direction, upward past the high ankles, rambling lewdly like a roaming ne'er-do-well, to the hollows of the knees. And from there, as soon as she bent down—which, with her height, was often necessary—a little bit higher, to the rising hem of her dress; never as far as the middle of her body, because the path from the floor to halfway up her thighs was long enough and lasciviously, horrifyingly magnificent.

In a word, for Kutian Mitzi was Mona Belinda again, the virgin who had been sawed into two halves. He could not encompass her from top to bottom with a single glance; she transcended any measurement, any human field of view. He saw only either her head and breasts, like the wax dummies in the windows of hair salons, or the trained, elegant set of legs. The piece in between, for the sake of which men in general, depending on their disposition, look into women's faces or at their legs, remained taboo for Kutian.

He did not even dare look when—God knows how—nature's blind motivating force had accomplished its never changing purpose in the darkness of the nights, and things had gone as they usually go when a man and a woman must live together almost skin to skin in a dwelling that is too small.

To possess the beautiful Mitzi was desecration. And that such a small, bow-legged fellow was permitted to desecrate this goddess with impunity provided him with lascivious pleasure, but he did not dare watch himself commit this sin. In the daytime he hardly dared speak to her and remained as before the inferior, incidental bed visitor, the thief who had sneaked into the anteroom of the temple to savor at night his false victories over the holy statue.

And after that had all taken place, the Mona Belinda of the past also could not forgive the Mitzi of today. Slowly, as always much too slowly—even later she probably did not become clearly conscious of it, but in the flat hollows of her soul that dreamed away like ponds a vile feeling filled with foreboding hazily arose, muddy ground water swarming with repulsive creatures. And she experienced her life at that time as a swamp. Slowly, ruminating for weeks, she extracted the past from that swamp:

Love, red, risky undertaking, magnificent danger of being eaten up.

Marriage, degradation, as a harbor of refuge against immoderation.

And now prostitution. Neither passion nor reason had been present during this indiscriminate response to necessity.

And then she began to take revenge on Kutian. When he once dared to ask her about the origin of her strange scar, she answered, "Someone attacked me. I didn't want to, but he was stronger than I was. . ." And her glance left no doubt about the fact that this stronger individual's act of violence and cruelty still meant more to her today than Kutian's caresses.

"Do you want a life like mine?" Anna asked when she noticed that Mitzi's belly began to grow maternally round. Mitzi seemed to be hardly listening; she was often absent-minded now, but in any case she did not contradict when the old woman continued: "It will be best if you marry Kutian."

Then she took Kutian to task.

"It isn't mine at all," he tried to talk his way out of it. "The one who gave her the scar is probably the father."

"The scar? She has the scar because I was frightened when I was pregnant. I made a mistake and struck myself on the cheek and the neck; she already had the red mark there when she was born."

"She told me herself that she was attacked and..."

He was in a turmoil and he wanted to release the fury of his suppressed jealousy on Mitzi.

"If you don't want to marry her, you can go," said Anna unmoved. It was a lie and blackmail, but in her experience more could be achieved with that than with sincerity and gentleness.

The Lainz Animal Refuge is actually a section of free landscape, a ridge with woods, meadows, and forest paths, surrounded by a wall, of course, whose gates are shut at night, but still large enough as an excursion area. You cannot get lost in it; the paths are marked. On Sundays they are flooded with tourists, but on weekdays it is very quiet there, and if you slowly stroll along the lonely forest paths, it can happen that suddenly, with a loud rustling of the bushes, a stag will dash past, mighty and crowned with antlers. Or you check your stride at the edge of a clearing and stand before a young buck deer with its fine crown of antlers above the soft and haughty forehead with its infinitely affected bearing. The buck freezes, then turns with his sniffing little muzzle away from the coarse, loud, disreputable human being, but he has no real fear because he knows that he is protected. Slowly and coldly he disappears into the brush, and you think that you hear the voice from the fairy tale ring out: "He who drinks from me will become a deer. . ."

But deer could even become angels more easily than the bow-legged body that stood gnarled and bent by the burden of existence at the edge of the clearing could become a deer, a creature of such lightness and silky reservedness.

Besides, the monster at the edge of the forest could not appreciate the animal's beauty; he was only thinking what a pity it was that one could not set a trap here because gamekeepers unceasingly circled the terrain with their bicycles.

Kutian's mouth watered at the thought of a larded venison roast au jus. He could probably make a usable snare out of wire, but a deer was too large. You could probably hide a wild piglet under your coat and throw it over the wall at a certain place, then walk decently out the main gate and go back for the prize unnoticed later. Of course, for that you could not use a normal wire snare. You had to use a real steel trap that killed when it closed, because the piglets had penetrating cries, and if one began to squeal, the entire pack would rush away with squeals and grunts, and the dull thud-thud-thud of the short, straight peg-legs against the forest ground would alarm the guards who would be here with their bicycles more quickly than you could cut the captured animal's throat, hide the precious trap, and get away.

The confinement of the animals here was easy, the freedom of the human being, on the other hand, that questionable freedom to starve undisturbed, was difficult. There were simply too many people, many more than the animals that were becoming more scarce.

People were no rarity, at least people such as Kutian: that was nothing rare.

This thought led him back to the misery of his life. Mitzi began to make herself scarce. She did not want him any more. That enraged him, especially because he never found the courage to use force against her. One ought to catch this overly tall, cool-eyed woman with her white, arrogant flesh in a wire snare so that she could no longer resist because in so doing she would strangle herself, and then—and then. . . !

His eyes glistened. With hands that trembled with longing but carefully took hold out of cruelty of will, he set up the lethal trap in the brushwood of the wild boar's trail and began to watch. He had stolen this trap from the scrap-metal dealer's storage yard, removed the rust, and repaired it. For his purposes it was actually much too large.

But he knew too little about poaching and about setting up traps. The animals seemed to catch his scent or to be warned by something else. They came trotting up through the undergrowth from far away; he already thought he could hear their sniffing; then it was suddenly quiet, and then they turned in another direction. Kutian finally feared that the forest keepers could come past here on their rounds and find him suspicious. People of his stamp were always suspicious to people of their sort. He decided to leave and to return two hours later. But just when he came back, one of the gamekeepers was standing around on the path quite near the place, and so Kutian walked slowly on. He sensed that the guard followed him with his eyes, and he had hardly taken a hundred decently strolling strides when he was overtaken by the man on his bicycle. He rode ahead of him to the lane. There he turned around and rode back, throwing a sharp glance at him as he did.

Had his trap perhaps already been discovered? Kutian became afraid and angrily got out of there.

When he sought out the place again the next day, the trap was nowhere to be seen. Either it had already been discovered and taken away, or he had not committed the place to memory precisely enough after all. Perhaps there was also a hidden watcher crouching here somewhere in the shrubbery, waiting to catch him red-handed. Kutian took out a paper cup and walked through the surrounding area under the pretext of looking for strawberries. But the more often he thought that he had now found the right place, the more questionable his sense of orientation became, and finally he had to give up. The trap that he had stolen with so much craftiness and so skillfully repaired was gone.

With its help perhaps someone else would soon cover his table with tasty morsels. That embittered Kutian terribly, but he did not yet think of further consequences.

The boy had become five years old, and, as was appropriate for his limited strength, he had not yet extended his expeditions far beyond the immediate vicinity. At that time he had not yet discovered the zoo. For some time his grandmother had been taking him along every day up onto the hill where she could keep an eye on him from the sales booth.

On this day, however, out of pure obstinacy he had seized a favorable opportunity to walk home. He had wanted to stay home and, through incessant whiny pestering, force his mother to play with him. His mother was ill, as she had so often been lately. Ill—that is, she lay in bed in a strange apathy and reacted neither to the grandmother's scolding nor her pleas. In such circumstances the father was nothing more to her than a target that had been caused to hop around joltingly by her cheap mechanism, the kind that you see in shooting and throwing galleries. Silently, she shot a glance down at him now and then from her round eyes, and then the target stood spellbound, tipped over, began to moan, or even broke into tears from the unsteadiness of his drunken condition, and then with a last, dying rattle became silent again. It was not without reason that the mother had called him a "shooting gallery target doll." She had hardly gotten some peace in that fashion when she fell into apathy again. Her gaze strayed away from Kutian, something soft and floating came into her face, and she sank into herself. After that, Kutian had lately begun to rattle empty bottles around, cursing loudly and throwing provoking glances at her. If she did not acknowledge him, he directed questions at her in domineering tones: Was she crazy?! Did she consider him to be a moron?! Nothing but questions that would actually have required an exclamation point at the end, but, because his courage left him at the last moment, were quickly provided with a meekly softening question mark. If it had been left up to Kutian, he would have screamed at her, perhaps even hit her. But it was not left up to Kutian. Everyone in the house knew that.

Little Josef understood only this much about the trouble between the two of them: His father was afraid of his mother. And because he was so glad to see his father in that nasty situation, at such moments he especially loved his mother. He pushed his way to her, whined around, and demonstrated to his father how much more his mother put up with from him, for in her presence his father did not dare hit him. Usually the scene ended with Kutian leaving angrily to go get drunk somewhere. Then the boy would creep up to his mother's bed. He pressed his rachitic child's belly against the edge of the bed, pouted, begged, flared up impatiently, or tugged at her hair. Basically, this misbehavior and the penetrating impertinence of his solicitation simply gave voice to the deepest and most hopeless loneliness, and as much as he otherwise and with respect to everyone else asserted his right to that isolation—as to a possession that he did not want to let be diminished by their curiosity and intrusiveness—here, before his mother, who had removed herself ever deeper into a white emptiness, he felt that her indifference was lonely, like a snow-covered peak above green land. His loneliness, on the other hand, was no privilege and no possession, but a dull, hopelessly black burden. So sharply did the white loneliness of the sick woman who loved nobody stand in contrast to the black loneliness of the one whom nobody loved.

In general he despised the occasional kindness of the adults who behaved as though they were doing him a favor with it. But he craved the kindness of his mother. He thirstily sucked in every word, every glance from her, and when she condescended to play with him, he degenerated into a kind of frenzy of carrying things too far, he squealed and made a clown of himself, he wanted so desperately to please her and break through that hated, white wall that took her more and more away from him. He had the thoroughly correct opinion that she was gradually freezing solid, and he doubled his hectic efforts to lure her back out of herself, at which he alone sometimes briefly succeeded. To be sure, his grandmother drove him away even more zealously than his jealous father, for she believed that his mother was ill and needed rest, but he knew better. She was not ill at all; she had no fever like he did when he was sick, as seldom as that was; on the contrary, she became colder and colder.

Only with stubborn resistance had he let himself be dragged along by the old woman to the hill that day, but he had soon escaped from her again and was now slowly trotting homeward over the concrete squares of the sidewalk, between the monotonous, clean, newly built houses and the roundly clipped maple trees. The heat was cripplingly tiring, but like all those for whom trouble and affliction have become natural at an early age, the five-year-old was already stoically submitting himself to the pressure of the pre-thunderstorm heat, the bites of the flies, the sting of the sun, and the dull pain of weariness in his ankles; he was submitting himself while he thoughtlessly trotted onward at a rather constant speed. As long as you did not think about them, weariness, affliction, heat, hunger, or frost could hardly be felt; you simply had to refrain from stopping at all to rest, which would have made the difference; and you could not slow down, otherwise the way became endless.

Only when he stepped into the cool driveway did he stop, wipe the sweat from his face, and rub his dusty toes alternately on the ankle of the other foot. At the end of the driveway the gate stood halfway open, and in the square opening, as though garishly and artificially painted on a stage, he saw the magnificent colors of the garden. A distant paradise, preserved behind glass, seemed to glow in from there. For some seconds it seemed to the boy as though he had been fast asleep and had now awakened with a dazed mind from the heat of brewing dreams. The garden back there had such an irreal glow. In the casklike vault of the cool entryway he thought that he could hear the spiders weaving their webs, it was so still there. And he stood there, small, lost, and empty.

Suddenly he was afraid, as if something were lurking and watching him from somewhere, something large, black, with an open mouth. Now he felt it behind his back. It breathed silently on him, causing the hair on the back of his neck to stand up. With a crackle, the bristling crept higher to the crown of his head. His scalp stretched coldly and was suddenly too tight for him.

He fled into the lightless space in front of the apartment door and slammed the iron gate shut behind him, so that the black thing with its wide-open mouth could not come in behind him, but the door went bang, and then it raised a drawn-out, demented creaking and very slowly opened again.

As though driven, he plunged into the kitchen and from there with a single bound into the other room—and there he froze in wonder, for after the horror came something that was incomprehensibly wonderful, like in a fairy tale:

On the bed his mother lay stretched out in the radiant whiteness of her bare skin. The long, bright legs hung to the side, loosely crossed over the edge of the bed; her toenails glowed red. She had nothing on but panties of silvery leaves and a similar bra. Her left arm was propped up on its elbow and bore the graceful length of her raised upper body. Her gaze simultaneously had something deeply weary and something uncontrollably wild in it, and her scar was reddishly flushed as it always was when she was very agitated. In one hand she held a red apple that she contemplated with a very unusual expression. Her eyes glowed with gorgeous insanity.

"Mother!" the boy whispered uneasily. "Mother. . . will you play with me, Mother?"

She seemed not to notice him; she did not turn her glance away from the apple for an instant. But after a while she moved her lips in a murmur.

"Tiger," she said, and then more and more rapidly: "Tiger, tiger, tigertigertiger. . ."

Suddenly she threw the apple violently toward where the boy was standing. He reached into the air, for now it was clear that this was a new game, a kind of ball game, but he missed the apple and rushed after it on all fours under the second bed. There he seized the apple with his teeth to fetch it for her like a dog. And she laughed at that, she who could almost never laugh because, too dull to grasp the quickly comical, she usually got stuck in the early stage of laughter, the surprise. She laughed clattering and shouting.

"Tiger!" she shouted merrily. "My little tiger, come, jump on me and bite me!"

Overcome with joy, he lost control of himself, sprang with a bound onto her belly, so that he sat astride her and held her between his knees, let the apple drop, and threw his arms around her neck. With his pent-up need for love, with the cruel ardor of neglected souls he attacked her, with kisses and bites and stammering exuberance.

"My little Bengal tiger," she whispered tenderly and pressed him to her, and finally he curled up comfortably at her breast and slept.

But when the grandmother came home and approached the bed, Mitzi began to hiss and to rant and to make insane noises, and the hospital attendants who finally came and got her needed their entire strength and skill to unwind the boy from her arms unharmed and to put her in the straitjacket.

After Mitzi had vanished from his life to lead a completely unknown, mysterious life of her own behind bars in a cell, alone with thoughts, feelings, and memories to which his impotent jealousy had no access, Kutian drank every day.

He suspected that the insanity that had befallen her in some way had something to do with the unknown rival who had given her the scar. The scar and perhaps also the child. She had returned to him; she had him with her in the insane asylum; the nights were filled with him; her strange dreams revolved around him.

Kutian, however, that minor character far down in the sediment of her extraordinary fate, crept up her legs in vain like a dung beetle, to the hollows of her knees. He got no further, even in his imagination; again and again she brushed him off with a casual flick of her hand and left him lying on his back, helplessly kicking his legs. When he visited her in the hospital, she did not even recognize him. Her gaze wandered indifferently past him.

It was only little Josef that she usually recognized immediately.

In the room, the Sunday morning stillness hummed. Of the woman who sat on the terrace in the wicker chair, one could see only the slender, well-formed legs and a strip of the flowered dressing gown. Everything else was covered by the newspaper that she held with both hands in front of her, with her elbows propped up on the arms of the chair. Like trim plastic clothespins at the same height on the right and the left, her fingernails grasped the edge of the newspaper and held it up. They were pale pink, impeccably manicured, and not too long. The upper edge of the newspaper trembled barely visibly now and then. By that one could tell that she—she had sat there silently and motionlessly for half an hour—was still alive behind her newspaper.

When he picked up his hat from the table, she lowered the newspaper a little, only enough to enable her eyes to look out across the white edge with the somewhat fixed gaze of the near-sighted person. At that moment it seemed to him that as long as he had known her she had always held some paper prop printed with current phrases in front of her, while only now and then casting a watchful glance at him over the top of it. She reminded him of his mother. Every time he had wanted to enjoy himself by doing something stealthily and quietly, perhaps take a peach from the fruit bowl on the credenza without asking, he had immediately felt his mother's eyes resting on him, no matter how involved she was in conversation or handiwork. And then it came—not the prohibition, not at all—only that unavoidable spoiling of his fun with restrictive rules: "But wash it first!"

Melitta was also like that. Her gaze fleetingly expressed displeasure, of course, because he was about to go out without telling her where or asking her to come along. But no prohibition followed. She only said, "But be back for dinner at one o'clock sharp!" and disappeared again behind the printed page.

Uncertainly he went out and stopped in front of the garage. He had wanted to go for a drive, but she had spoiled his fun. He clasped his hands behind his back, a posture that was actually uncomfortable because he had to shove his belly forward in assuming it, but one that he had unconsciously adopted from his boss. Then he marched down the street like an old professor who wants to get a little exercise before dinner. Mechanically he took the path to the back entrance of the castle park, strolled along between exotic trees and bushes, now and then absent-mindedly read the Latin inscription on one of the name plates, and wound up in front of the zoo.

The flamingos bloomed like pinkish white bouquets of feathery carnations above the shallow pond surrounded with concrete. Black swans, regal frigates of mourning, sailed past. The screeching of the parrots, whose cages had been hung in the open air, irritated him like a malicious nuisance. He pressed more quickly past the volaries toward the predator cages.

He found the attendant sitting on a wooden stool in front of his quarters. He too had the Sunday newspaper in front of him, but was not reading it. It hung loosely, half folded together in his left hand, and his gaze roamed comfortably out across it to the colorful crowd. He immediately recognized the doctor and stood up politely when the latter stopped in front of him and seemed inclined toward a short conversation, one that unexpectedly became longer because between the two men of approximately the same age, without regard for social and intellectual differences, after just a few sentences, that unspoken congeniality appeared that occurs almost exclusively between men: the feeling of pleasant partnership, at a respectful distance from any familiarity, far away from that boundary beyond which friendships and enmities are possible.

The contemplative conversation, interrupted by many pauses, was continued as they wandered through the lanes, for the attendant had to make his rounds, and the doctor now actually said that he had wanted to get some more exercise before dinner anyway, and accompanied him. He asked about the little Kutian boy and then gave a detailed elaboration of the desolate impressions that he had received in the boy's home.

"What an environment!" he said while shaking his head. And then he was irritated because with those words he saw himself using an expression and a tone of voice that was typical for Melitta. "Horrifying social conditions," he therefore continued in his own words. "What will become of such a child?"

"He's difficult to train, that's certain," said the attendant. "But he's useful for the work here and willing to do it. Perhaps later I can train him to be an animal keeper. The animals like him."

"You take a serious interest in the boy?" the doctor asked. "Then I must make you aware of something. I'm afraid he has a hereditary defect. His mother has already spent a year with us in the mental hospital."

"So, then she's. . ." The attendant tapped his forehead. "Is it curable? Can't such a thing be cured these days?"

"Under certain circumstances. There are methods that bring a high percentage of cures."

"What kind of methods are those?" the attendant politely asked, to give the doctor the opportunity for a conversation in which his knowledge far surpassed that of his partner.

"Electroshock, insulin shock. Then there are also the possibilities of hypnosis. Prolonged hypnotic sleep. . ."

"I understand a little bit about that," the attendant modestly interjected. "I used to be an animal trainer."

Klingengast smiled patronizingly, but the fairness that prevailed between them now caused him to use attentive glances and questions to stimulate the attendant to talk about his own special field as well.

"It also has something to do with hypnosis," said the attendant. "To be sure, you don't put the animals, but rather the wild part of them into a kind of sleep. There they can move normally, eat, and jump, and in general do everything that they can do in their waking condition, but they actually have a kind of sleeping cap on. For they can't do what they really want; they can't be wild animals, free to tear and kill. They've forgotten that they want it. That part sleeps. Of course it doesn't sleep very deeply. 'Stead o' that they have to be tame and do what the trainer wants."

'Stead o' that, Klingengast thought. Instead of that is more correct, to be sure, but it sounds very prosaic. How colorful such dialect usages can be: 'stead o' that—'stead o' wanting, as if wanting were an independent agency, a kind of second personality. . .

"Hypnosis and shock," he said in agreement. "Influence and whip."

"Those who work with the whip and with the prod, or even with burning, are crude dilettantes. I never did that. Of course, you have to be very strong. First you have to train your body until you have it in hand.

Until you're no longer afraid of anything. When you've lost all fear, you begin to have inner power. That too must be trained for a long time. You draw your will very tightly together, just as you do your muscles, and then you let it fly. It comes out of your eyes in the form of rays and grabs the animal."

He had illustrated the drawing together of the will with both hands by balling them to fists, and then suddenly, spreading all of his fingers, thrusting them away from his body toward the imaginary animal.

"What you just performed there is the motion that the gypsies use to curse someone," said the doctor thoughtfully. "It's an ancient magical gesture. Your training has something to do with black magic."

"That's quite possible," the attendant answered.

For a while he walked silently along next to the other man, and suddenly he began to speak again with a changed voice, more softly than before, making an effort to formulate something that he himself did not yet really understand.

"I had great power over the animals."

And after a reflective pause he seemed to have given up the idea of expressing himself. "The devil take it," he simply murmured. "To fail once is to fail always."

"Did you have to give up your profession because of a failure?" asked Klingengast.

"Yes."

They walked on to the next tree. Then the attendant said, "One day you come with your magic, as you call it, to one that is stronger. And then you lose your confidence. And then it's over."

"The stronger one. . . who was that in your case? Everyone meets someone stronger sometime, you know."

"It was a woman. Eve in the Garden of Eden. It would have become our best routine. I was Adam. I had thought out a wonderful number and had to do all of the hard work alone. She simply lay there. She was beautiful, to be sure, very beautiful. But the animals don't understand that. They ate from her hand only because I commanded them to. She, on the other hand, she didn't want to. She didn't eat out of my hand. . . I don't like to think about it, Doctor."

At the attendant's first words, the physician had given a short dry laugh.

"Eve," he said and nodded his head vigorously. "Of course, nature. That woman! Simply lies there, and we have to do all of the hard work and bang our heads against a wall. We have hardly dissected her body and unveiled it when she plays a trick on us and has a soul, so to speak. We call it the psyche. To be sure, we've also succeeded in learning something about this psyche, but not very much yet. I suspect that quite different depths and devilments are still lying beneath what we've discovered until now."

"I'll tell you what's beneath it," said the attendant. "I mean, of course, what was beneath it in my case: an uninfluenceable block. Nothing. Emptiness. Nothing at all. You fail when you encounter that."

"Are you an atheist?" asked Klingengast.

"You mean, am I godless? No. . . why do you ask? That is, I've never thought about it. I don't know."

"I've thought about it," said Klingengast. "I don't know either. But now I must go. I have to be home at one for dinner."

He was at home at one o'clock sharp, just as he had been told. The table was set for three people; they were expecting his mother for dinner. She arrived a minute after him, and he met her at the door as always, kissed her hand, and led her to the table where Melitta and he stood politely behind their chairs until the old lady had sat down.

As a boy he had secretly loved her, for she had been beautiful, and her perfectly formed, ladylike confidence had made her infinitely superior. At the same time he had feared her unwearyingly observing gaze. There was nothing that would have escaped that gaze, no thread on a suit, no uncertainty in tone of voice if he lied to her, and not the fresh scrape on his knee that revealed to her that he had climbed over the garden wall again to get his ball because he was too lazy to run into the house for the key to the iron gate that was locked even in the daytime. To be sure, she seldom criticized him, for she was aware of the weakened impact of punishments that were given too often, but she never failed to let him know that she registered every misdeed. The silent reprimand of her glance shamed him and did not fail to have its effect. I have given up, that gaze seemed to say. This child is hopeless. And then he also felt hopeless.

Later he had begun to watch her as well, and it had not escaped him that she too had flaws. At first he was very alarmed about that; then it had given him quiet satisfaction, and finally, crippling and humiliating for him as for her, it had turned into sympathy. He had long since ceased to fear her; she was too old and fragile, and her feeble, somewhat lengthened way of speaking, with the quietly hissing "ch," had taken on a whiny tone since her son's sympathy had become the final position from which she could dominate him. He could have resisted that, for he saw through the trick, but he was simply the type that voluntarily remains in the cage out of rational considerations, even when the door is open. He knew too much about the necessity of all limitations of freedom. His patients had broken out, and it was his task to lead them carefully back into the humane cages from the still much more terrible freedom that they had gotten into. In general however, he loved them more than the normal people, more than his family, for they never bored him. They were interesting, and they belonged to him. They needed him.

Sunk in such thoughts, he emptied his soup dish while the two ladies made conversation. Now and then a word penetrated his absent-mindedness. They were talking about something that had been in the newspaper that morning. It did not interest him and was of no concern to him. But then a name rang in his ear. He pricked up his ears.

"But of course!" said his mother plaintively. The "ch's" hissed softly as though she were saying (in German) *Ischbittdisch.* "Of course it was him. He doesn't have an alibi! After all, every decent person has an alibi!"

Melitta raised her eyes and focused them automatically on the tiny spot in the table cloth that had been made where Klingengast had laid the used soup spoon next to his empty dish.

To be sure, Melitta's opinions were similar to those of his mother, but she had a mind that was capable of greater objectivity.

"An alibi," she said thoughtfully, "proves something. No alibi still doesn't prove anything."

"But of course it does. Who else could it have been?" the old woman moaned in indignation. "They say he's a little, bow-legged fellow, an unemployed man as well, and besides that a notorious drinker, unstable and reprobate! I really ask myself, where do the people get the money to drink when they're unemployed?"

"I say the same thing!" Melitta emphatically agreed. Her correct High German seemed more honest and more pleasant to him than the affected diction of his mother, who spoke Viennese only because in her time it had been considered elegant. (*Ischbittdisch*, even the emperor had spoken dialect.)

"A person like that is no better than an animal," said Melitta.

That was the verdict. Irrefutable. Inexorable.

"How crude people are!" moaned old Mrs. Klingengast. "I ask you! To catch a young girl that way in a rusty trap and then. . . no, they say that he mauled her, well, it's simply hor-ri-ble!"

"Hor-ri-ble!" Melitta confirmed with beautiful calmness. "But the death penalty has been done away with, of course. And who are the victims? We helpless women."

She spoke without affectation. It was clear that she did side with the helpless women, but that she did not at all include herself among them. Sex murders! Such a thing could not happen to her. Again her gaze wandered expressionlessly and nevertheless provokingly to the damp spot in the table cloth. Next to it, Klingengast laid his fork, dripping with juice from the roast, and looked up triumphantly. But he had apparently made a mistake. She said nothing about it; she seemed not to have noticed it. Then he felt childish. But perhaps that was also simply one of her tricks.

"Besides that, he also has a child," Melitta said, shaking her head.

The old lady carefully let the juice run off of a piece of the roast before she laid it on her plate.

"I ask you, must such people also have children besides?"

"Nice genotype," Melitta observed. "The father a sex murderer, the mother mentally ill. What do you think about that?" she said, turning to her husband.

"I?" Klingengast murmured. "I didn't hear what you were talking about."

"About the Kutian case, of course. The wife is supposed to be with you in the Rose Hill Clinic."

"No wonder, with such a husband," the old lady bitterly interjected, as if it were her own husband.

"Do you know the woman?" Melitta suddenly asked alertly and disregarded her mother-in-law's comment as the inappropriate sentimentality of a maudlin old woman.

"No," said Klingengast, feeling the pressure. He simply did not want to talk with the two women about the case.

But it was not shock because the name that he had earlier thought he heard unclearly had now actually been spoken, it was anger that changed his voice, suppressed, but immediately rising violently again, anger at the way the two women, between the soup and the roast, transformed the terrible fate of strangers in their conversation, at how they condemned deeds about whose motivations they, in their sheltered world, could know nothing and did not even want to know anything. After all, it concerned living, feeling people, people whom he knew! Well, perhaps the difference in their way of looking at the matter also lay only in that, in the accidental fact that they did not know them, while he saw before him the real Kutian instead of the abstract Kutian case.

He had to think of the grandmother, whose vegetable garden now seemed to him like a symbol for everything that such people had originally expected from life: simply to live, eat, sleep, work, and then pass on the whole thing, that simple task of existence, to the next rising generation. But that was not granted to these simple, peace-loving people. Like a rending tiger, fate had broken into their poor little garden, their everyday existence.

But here sat others who also basically wanted nothing but to live, eat, sleep, and procreate—even though with somewhat higher pretensions—and who, in the face of all that was just, had succeeded; sat here and gaped at misery or crime or illness and enjoyed it at their leisure besides, because between their world and the evil animal fate there were protecting bars: happiness, wealth, position, education, morality. And arrogance. The arrogance of those who had neither the opportunity nor the necessity—and also would not have had enough courage and strength at all to become animals themselves in the battle with the animal.

"So you don't know her, that. . . person?" Melitta repeated her question, and now there was no longer any doubt: Mrs. Kutian, the "person" whom Klingengast had denied knowing, was Melitta's enemy. For to her greatest amazement she discovered that her husband had just lied to her. He never lied otherwise. Was it necessary for him to lie to her, to her who understood everything and with whom he could talk reasonably about everything? It alarmed her. Where had he been this morning? Where, on that Sunday when he had justified his tardiness with the sprained ankle of some street urchin? She had already had a warning feeling then. And now she was perfectly certain that he was lying, for she had posed her question only as a trap. That morning, because the new sex murder had aroused her curiosity, she had already called the clinic and learned that Mrs. Kutian was even lying in the ward in which her husband worked. Of course she was too polite to say it to his face, but she had to let him know: You can't lie to me. I'm not as childish and stupid as your mother!

"Of course not, in such a huge hospital! He can't know everyone, you know!" the old lady murmured in conclusion and stood up. The conversation was exhausted; it was sated with the roast, sated with horror; she longed to take her usual afternoon nap.

Obediently and enthusiastically Klingengast carried two deck chairs into the garden for the women and set them up in the shade.

He too wanted to lie down for a while, not in the garden, but in a darkened room, but he could not calm down. The conversation had stirred him up and put him in a mood of panic: It was high time that somebody intervened here and averted the calamity that rolled feelinglessly onward, beneath which an entire family would be crushed. And who else was more obligated to intervene than he, who stood far enough away from the events to grasp them clearly, who stood on an intellectual plane high above such misfortunes and blunders, and into whose hands chance had given all of the threads on which the individual actors of the drama fidgeted as helplessly as marionettes? They seemed to him to exemplify calamity itself, the indissoluble amalgamation and interaction of misfortune and guilt.

Resolutely he got up again. There was someone who could help him in this task. The feeling of silent partnership that had touched him so pleasantly that morning quietly and comfortingly returned.

On the way to the zoo, his mind worked out a plan that should bring about the best possible solution for the family members who could still be saved. It was one of those schematic solutions, patent medicines of the kind that enlightened reason holds ready for all situations of life: He would speak with Kutian's attorney. Kutian had to be examined regarding his mental condition. He could obtain a place for the grandmother with his colleague in the municipal welfare home. Little Josef would be placed in a children's home.

The attendant greeted him as though he had expected him. He already knew everything, partially from the newspaper, partially from Josef who had come to the zoo as usual to help him with the feeding. The boy's report had been full of stoic equanimity and of the briefest form:

"My father's in jail. He killed a woman."

It did not depress him much, but another worry gnawed at his heart. Previously his father had visited his mother on Sundays in the insane asylum, and then sometimes he had taken the boy along, for they did not permit children go there alone. His grandmother never visited her daughter; she explained that she was too old to experience such things.

Klingengast immediately offered to take the boy with him to the institution, so that he could see his mother, to whom he seemed very attached in spite of her mental condition. And the attendant wanted to come along as well. He had already involuntarily assumed the role of a substitute father for the boy.

She was no longer violent. She simply lay there in the striped linen smock, indolent and apathetic. She had grown very fat, and her head now seemed even smaller on the massive body. Her skin exhibited the diaphanous, somewhat greasy whiteness that one can see in nuns whose faces are seldom exposed to the sun and bright daylight. On the whole, she gave the impression of an enormous soft-bodied reptile, an oversized cave salamander.

When Klingengast entered the cell with the attendant and the child, she did not react. She simply lay there, one arm propped up; her long, still beautiful legs were covered by the hospital smock to a point above the knees and were stretched to the side, loosely crossed, over the edge of the bed. Her hair was tousled, still glistening and elastic. Its thick curls swayed softly in the draft as the door was opened and then closed.

She turned her profile to the visitors, the crooked nose, the tiny mouth, and the chin that was now full and fat, passing almost without indentation into the high, broad, snow-white neck; the large, almond-shaped eye, drawn slanting over into the profile and following the high arc of the yoke bone, with its cold basilisk gaze beneath the somber arrow of the long eyebrow; and the scar, beginning thin at the yoke bone, as though drawn with a fine brush stroke, then curling forward in a few bulgingly thickened spirals over her cheek and neck, then, drawn thin and fine once more, disappearing between the broad breasts. This was no longer a woman; she was an extraordinary being, a cruel goddess of nature. They stood as though spellbound, breathing softly, peculiar pilgrims in the sanctuary of the serpent goddess.

Suddenly she turned her head with a swaying motion in which her neck did not seem to participate, while the white mask of her inhuman countenance still turned toward them and the longish eyes with their round pupils stared right through the trio without any sign of the recognition that would have meant, of course, something like acknowledgement of their existence. Slowly, a fear of this feelingless, gigantic doll crept up the back of the attendant's neck.

"You have visitors, dear Mrs. Kutian," said the doctor and in so doing raised his voice somewhat louder than usual. It was full of that artificially compelling optimism that he considered to be appropriate vis-à-vis his patients.

She did not answer. Her staring gaze went through the figures standing at the door and reduced them to fleeting patterns of not-quite-believable existence.

Klingengast turned to the attendant. "She isn't responsive," he explained. "She doesn't recognize anybody and doesn't speak. She always simply lies there impassively."

At that moment the boy ran to the sick woman.

"Mother!" he gasped, breathless with excitement. "You, look! I brought you something!"

He took a red apple out of his pocket and held it out to her. She looked at it sightlessly and gave no sign of joy or of understanding. Then he threw the apple in the air, caught it again, and moved it temptingly and invitingly back and forth in front of her face.

"Mother!" he begged. "You! Look here! Come on and play with me!"

Now her masklike face gradually came to life, the scar took on a darker color, as if new life were shooting into it and distributing itself slowly through the whole body that was drowsing away in a stupor. The tendons of her long toes twitched; her breasts rose with deeper breaths. The boy took the apple between his teeth and danced around her bed as though possessed, then with a bound he leaped upon her, remained lying astride her body, let the apple fall carefully into her lap, and threw his arms around her.

Beneath the attack of the wild youngster, she lay down laughing on her back and laughed monotonously and rather loudly for a while. But then the laughter broke off suddenly, and she turned her head toward Klingengast, for he had hurried over to tear the boy from her arms. He feared that the insane woman would have an incalculable reaction, perhaps even an attack of frenzy.

She had put her left arm around the boy and was pressing him tightly to her breast. Her face took on a brooding expression, her upper lip curled back revealing her teeth, and from her breast pressed a soft, warning growl.

The doctor wanted to reach for the boy, but the attendant had stepped up behind him and suddenly held him by both arms with an iron grip.

"What do you think you're doing?" said Klingengast softly. "The child must be taken away from her. He's in the gravest danger."

Her scar now burned fiery red and pulsated with ever new waves of still darker red, like the angrily discolored swelling of an agitated turkey's wattles.

"No," said the attendant just as softly. "She won't do anything to him because he's not afraid of her. As long as you have no fear, they don't do anything to you."

"We're not in a circus ring, but in an insane asylum, my dear friend!" said Klingengast furiously. It seemed to him that the attendant had treacherously attacked him from behind. He of all people! The man whom he had trusted as a confederate! But he nevertheless permitted himself to be pulled a few steps away from the bed, then voluntarily returned to the door. It had occurred to him that the alarm bell, with which he could call the hospital attendants to help him, was situated right next to the door. But before he could activate it, the boy straightened up unabashedly and pushed the insane woman's confining arm away from him. He took the apple, which had rolled onto the white linen cloth, into his hand, and full of assiduity, and as if the presence of the two men in the room were completely immaterial for him and his mother, this conspiring duality that was only concerned with itself, he said, "Do you want to eat it, Mother? Should I break it apart? I can do it with my hands. I'm strong, Mother."

But she paid no attention to him; rather she continued to stare at the doctor with hostile glances. She stretched her neck as if she intended to get up, and rocked her head irritably.

"Josef!" the attendant commanded softly. "Climb down and come here to me!"

The boy obeyed immediately, and the insane women permitted it to occur without intervening. The doctor opened the cell door the breadth of a slot. First he pushed the boy out through it and then, without taking his eyes off the patient, the attendant as well. Before he could leave the cell himself, she moved. Slowly she stretched her arm out long and pointed her finger at the door with a commanding gesture.

"You too," she said.

"Certainly, dear Mrs. Kutian," the doctor said soothingly with a calm voice. "I'm going now. Do you need anything else?"

"Get out!" she screamed, drawing her sharply bent arm toward her and again urging him forth with a violent gesture of dismissal.

"When you have a Bengal tiger for a lover," she said slowly and coldly, "you don't need the man who cleans out his stall."

It often happens that a coincidental word, the word of a person who has no right to say anything to you, even the word of a fool, meaninglessly aimed past reality, nevertheless finds its mark. Confusion has collected for a long time beneath a thin layer of consciousness. The playfully spoken word falls onto it like a stone, and the firm ground proves to be a swamp into which it sinks. So you begin to observe the suspicious spot, or to go around it. But at night your dreams circle around the dangerous place, then your daytime friends approach as hostile dream figures and throw new stones at the place where a first shock revealed the sore point. It would be better not to be familiar with it.

Klingengast had a dream similar to one that he had dreamed once before as a child: The table was set festively, and he lay appetizingly prepared on his mother's plate, but she pushed the plate away. He was very willing to be eaten by her; therefore he stood up, picked up the knife and the fork, and rowed across the tablecloth toward her on the plate, as though he were in a rowboat. "Mother," he said. "Eat me, please." But she absent-mindedly declined with the words: "Please, I really must watch my figure." At that moment he saw Melitta sitting at the other end of the table. Hastily and joyfully he rowed across to her and invited her to eat him. "But I can't eat with my fingers," she said, shrugging her shoulders. Then he offered her the knife and fork with which he had rowed. But she did not accept them. Rather, she directed a reproachful glance at the tablecloth, and to his horror he saw that he had left a trail of meat juice behind him while rowing. "Excuse me, Melitta," he said remorsefully. She did not answer, but simply looked at him with icy contempt. He tried to defend himself. "I didn't do it on purpose. Don't be so petty. After all, you're my wife and you must eat me."—"Well, then I could simply eat the tablecloth," she said coldly. But no matter what, he wanted to be eaten; it seemed to him that all happiness and the entire meaning of his life depended upon someone consuming him. Melitta's unfeeling countenance hurled him into despair. Finally it occurred to him that they had been expecting Mrs. Kutian to come to dinner today. Hopefully he turned his plate and rowed searchingly along the edge of the table. "Of course, she didn't come, that woman." said his mother. Once more he conceived of a final way out. "Perhaps the tiger from the zoo could be brought, so that he..." But at that moment both women jumped up angrily and screamed, "There isn't one, there's no tiger!" He wanted so badly to have his way that with the power of his desire he gave the dream a twist in his favor: The door sprang open, and an enormous Bengal tiger marched in. It went up to the table, courteously placed its front paws on the tablecloth, and said with a squeaking child's voice, "I've had enough to eat, I don't want any meat." He remembered that this sentence had been in a book of fairy tales and protested, "I'm really not a little boy any more!" But the two women pointed at him, laughing loudly in derision, and he looked down at himself and discovered that he was wearing the Kutian boy's baggy pants. He awoke bathed in perspiration.

The moment he woke up he remembered the entire dream and decided to write it down and analyze it. But when he had gotten up and shaved, everything was already forgotten, and only a crippling feeling remained, as if he had forgotten something terribly important, something, however, that everyone else remembered.

Had Melitta really changed recently? She was so silent, but she had never been talkative. She had always had something coolly reserved and watchful about her, but now she seemed intent on making it her only task not to let him out of her sight for a second. From her glance spoke neither anxiety—although he actually did look pale and overworked—nor jealousy, tenderness, or fear. If one could attribute to such carefully controlled expressionlessness any feeling content at all, then it was most nearly contempt. In any case, he thought that he read contempt in her eyes, together with the desire to ferret out evidence of his despicableness and to lay that as plunder at the feet of her self-righteousness. She had always liked to elevate herself in the humiliation of others.

Even for her I am only someone "who cleans out the stall," he thought.

Instinctively he longed for the society of people whose sympathy expressly confirmed his worth, or for those who needed help and challenged and activated his power through their demands. He spent more time with his patients than would have been necessary, and he made it a constant habit to remain at home only at mealtimes on free days.

Soon he was drawn to the place where he thought the little boy would be, who needed his help if he wanted to see his mother; or to the attendant—although the feeling of having a respectful partner in this man had been shaken in a manner that he did not quite grasp, when he had felt the hard hands on his body, as they limited him in his freedom, held him fast, and hindered him in doing what he thought was right. But he wanted all the more to convince himself again of that man's deferential and benevolent attitude.

A feeling of relief overcame him when he saw in the attendant's eyes the honest joy at seeing him, and their very first words confirmed and renewed the peculiar, unspoken, and pleasant relationship between the two men.

"I'm pleased that you've come, Doctor! You must help me. As you know, they put little Josef in an orphanage, but he immediately ran away again, and I'm afraid that if they catch him, he'll be placed in a home for problem children, and there he'll become much more unhappy. Unhappy and angry. I want to adopt the boy, or at least assume responsibility for him. Can you tell me if that's possible and how it could be done?"

"Of course I can advise and help you there. But have you really considered what it is that you intend to bring into your home? It's always risky to raise a child of strangers, for one never knows how the child will develop, and in this case. . ."

"Doctor, I know exactly what I am taking upon myself. Josef will probably never become a completely normal human being. He will always remain a peculiar and not harmless animal. Perhaps, however, for that very reason nobody will be able to deal with him as well as I can. And I also have another reason. Since the little boy turned up here, a memory that I have turned this way and that for years, and one that has always tortured me, has begun to take on meaning. And actually, more than anything else it was that memory that I wanted to relate to you, if it will not bore you."

"You don't bore me at all," said Klingengast warmly. "How would it be if we drank a glass of wine up there in the Tirol House, while you tell me what you have on your mind?"

The attendant gladly consented, and they stepped out into the spacious castle park and walked along the quiet wooded paths to the tavern, where they sat down at a primitive wooden table under the trees and ordered wine. And the attendant began to tell his story.

Mona Belinda, the lady who was sawed in two every evening by her father the magician, and then put together again, had been about twenty years old when the trainer came to the circus with a group of animals that belonged to him. She was a magnificent sight to behold, a beauty with that rigid, expressionless solemnity to which stupidity makes an undeniable but positive contribution, a wondrous, conceited woman of fabulous height, who strutted around stiffnecked and round-eyed. Her thin, little, downward-curving nose resembled a beak; her mouth was small with corners that turned downward in vexation. Nothing ever transpired on her symmetrical face; it seemed to have solidified once and for all into a mask of amazement at its own beauty, insulted even by the idea that others could think differently.

Mona Belinda never laughed, and when she smiled, her little mouth twisted as though to weep. She was an unhappy creature, and as if she were aware of her stupidity, she was always ready to do what anyone else wanted of her, without thinking about it at all. Nevertheless, everything turned to misfortune for her, and she was successful at nothing but going on stage night after night and showing the public her beautiful, imposingly tall and slender body in a sequined leotard. After that she was placed in a box like a porcelain doll and sawed in two. The magician opened the one side of the box and showed the public Mona Belinda's flawless, long, sawed-off legs. Then he opened the other half of the box and revealed her upper body. Then both halves were closed and moved tightly together; the magician spoke strange words over them; and Mona Belinda climbed out of the case, rigid and solemn as when she climbed into it. Only her face still seemed to be amazed at the fact that her astonishing beauty had endured such an inhuman procedure unharmed. At that moment, after a breathless pause, the audience usually began to applaud and to allot to her for several minutes the admiration that was fitting for such an extraordinary creature. At her side the magician looked small and ordinary, and his bows of appreciation gave the impression that a brazen lackey was using the glory and fame of his mistress to put on airs.

But as soon as Mona Belinda had left the circus ring, her unusual height proved to be a hindrance to any happiness. She was too tall for the men. She could dance, but in a chorus line she would have towered by a head above all the other dancers. She would never have found a suitable dancing partner, and she lacked the temperament and ideas for a solo act. Mona Belinda was no artist. Her only exploitable talent consisted in remaining slender and flexible enough that she could roll herself together like a snake in one half of the box or the other as needed, while the magician showed the public the artificial legs that were housed in the false bottom, or the upper part of a wax doll that resembled her in every detail.

But she was not even granted a long career as a wax beauty sawed into two parts.

Mona Belinda loved the animals, perhaps because the monstrous quality of her beauty grew milder when she stood next to the giraffes and elephants instead of next to human beings of normal size. Even in the circle of animals that were constructed low to the ground, with snakes, apes, and predatory cats, she immediately gave the impression of being a natural divinity, and her inhuman dimensions became superhuman, almost divine proportions.

At least that is how she appeared to the young animal trainer. And then he had a marvelous idea about how to give the beautiful girl's performance in the circus the proper frame. He conceived a new act: Adam and Eve in the Garden of Eden, surrounded by the peaceful animals. He himself intended to appear as Adam, Mona Belinda would be Eve, and in order to conceal the difference in height, Eve would sit on a bed beneath the tree while he stood on a platform behind it, elevated, so that he could keep a careful eye on the animals while rising above Eve's horizontal splendor with his masculine, vertical height.

Since her father approved of the plan, Mona Belinda was willing to participate. But while they were rehearsing the new act, unforeseen difficulties arose: The animals did not like Mona Belinda, or so it seemed to the animal trainer at the time. They became agitated and restive the moment they were supposed to work in Mona Belinda's presence, and the animal trainer had to exert all of his suggestive power to keep them under control. After every rehearsal, he was streaming with perspiration from the concentration. It also seemed to him that a reduction of his suggestive abilities always went hand in hand with Mona Belinda's appearance in front of the cage or in the arena. That probably should have been enough warning for him, but he did not want to give up his plan. It injured his pride that dull animals resisted his will. His art consisted in the very fact that he had the ability to impose his will upon other creatures without using external force. Even with human beings he was a gifted hypnotist; especially with women he would have effortlessly achieved everything, if he had only wanted to do so, simply by using the commanding power of thoughts, that silent art of persuasion of his stronger spirit. The enjoyment that he drew from that, however, compensated him for the absence of more sensual pleasures, and he lived a chaste life.

Very slowly he accustomed the animals to Mona Belinda's statuesque presence. Grumbling and snarling they acquiesced, and when he had rehearsed the new act for the first time without any extraordinary safety measures, when for the first time the Bengal tiger, his ears trembling with resistance, submissively licked Mona Belinda's feet as he was commanded, and the shy antelope took the feed from her hand while the elephant, who was always good-natured, rocked his trunk over her and plucked the apple from the Tree of Knowledge with the tip of it, then threw it gently into her lap, a jubilant sense of increased power and heightened personality surged through the animal trainer.

Because of her godlike stupidity and indifference, Mona Belinda was not at all conscious of the danger and the brewing ill will of the animals. If she had been afraid, it would probably have been impossible to hold the animals in check in her presence, for they sense the fear of other creatures and usually take it as a signal for wildness that erupts unbridled. No layman could appreciate what a risk it was to let the antelope, whose most innate nature is quivering fear, sheer, uninterrupted fearful alertness, appear together with the predators.

But Mona Belinda's fearlessness extended not only to the predators, but also to the animal trainer. His demonic gaze, the magic of his will, the power of his masculinity—all of that slid off of her like water.

He had long since fallen prey to her abnormal beauty, but because of the exciting and exhausting work, he had not yet become aware of it at all. He loved Mona Belinda, but she rocked her long giraffe's neck high above him in wondering self-engrossment and responded to his glowing glances with the cool, round-eyed, conceited woman's gaze behind which everything and nothing may be concealed.

So finally, on that memorable evening, she led the way, entered the circus ring, bowed to the audience, and took her place beneath the Tree of Knowledge without even favoring it with a curious glance.

Then came the harmless animals; the antelope, a few monkeys, and the elephant trotted saluting and apathetically obedient around in a circle, then moved to their places, where they assumed the positions that they had rehearsed. They were followed by Adam with a pair of lions and the Bengal tiger.

When all of them were properly grouped, with the Bengal tiger crouching at Mona Belinda's white feet, the two lions rubbing flanks at her side, the antelope eating out of her outstretched hand, and the elephant—since a snake could not be trained to that extent—reaching for the apple with its snakelike trunk, the animal trainer looked at his Eve and wanted to catch her eye. She, however, looked indifferently at the audience, that mirror in which her own amazement was reflected a thousandfold, the grand triumph of her vanity in its craving for admiration. The animal trainer increased the internal pressure with which he sought to affect her. She did not react. A slight restlessness came over the animals. The elephant threw the apple into her lap too forcefully. It rolled out of her grasping hand and remained lying next to her in the sand. That was not anticipated.

She raised her eyes questioningly to the animal trainer, and he placed all of his imploring power in his gaze: she should leave the apple where it was; any unusual movement could disturb the animals. She still looked inquiringly at him. He repeated the silent command. Then she bent forward, reached for the apple, and as she did, her leg moved, seeking for balance, to a point right in front of the mouth of the tiger, who jerked back angrily and crouched down.

It did not happen at that moment. It did not happen until a second later, right at the moment when it became clear to the animal trainer that Mona Belinda could not be hypnotized. She did not feel his command, and that was what disturbed the animals: his weakness, not Mona Belinda's odor. For in her presence he had no will of his own and was weak. This realization was followed by a lightning-fast, reeling descent into fear and uncertainty. All of his power slipped away from him; he was nothing in the eyes of this beautiful doll; for seconds he ceased to exist.

The animals sensed it: The focus from which their movements and actions were directed dissolved into nothingness. Then they broke out.

The tiger struck once briefly.

Perhaps the trainer would have gotten control of his creatures again if this had been only a rehearsal. But it was the gala performance, the decisive performance before a thousand eyes that were directed at him and his defeat. The audience broke out in panicky screaming. Without the audience. . . perhaps. But "perhaps" is no platform from which you can keep your world in order.

He himself did not know how he had gathered up the blood-covered Mona Belinda from the ground and carried her to safety. Meanwhile, the tiger seized the antelope, the lions strode around hissing and slapping their tails in the sand, the elephant trumpeted loudly and trampled down the Tree of Knowledge. Showing presence of mind, the circus's stable boys raised the fall-gate that led from the arena into the lions' cage, and the remaining animals also fled back into their cages. The tiger remained in the ring as the great victor and began to eat the antelope.

When Mona Belinda had recovered, the animal trainer proposed marriage to her. Perhaps he had expected that the woman who was now disfigured by an ugly scar would be extremely happy. He definitely saw himself as a giver, not as someone who had to make amends for something. Nobody associated with the circus would have thought of viewing him as the guilty party who had destroyed her life, for danger and daring belong to such professions no differently than an official's profession requires him to go to the office even in bad weather. So the animal trainer's proposal was not at all presented as recompense for the misfortune that his plan had brought to Mona Belinda, but neither, for example, did sympathy because of her disfigurement play a role in it. For it was not her beauty, which was now severely diminished, but her unmoving, uninfluenceable nature that fascinated him as a symptom of powers that were much more than a match for his skills.

And since her father agreed to it, Mona Belinda indifferently said yes. She became a cold wife for the animal trainer. To be sure, she was not aware of any conscious resistance, but she also remained absolutely untamable during the course of their marriage. The animal trainer used his hypnotic gift on her just as fruitlessly as the spoken command. Although bent on doing everything right for him, she did not succeed because her stupidity and the infinitely sluggish reaction ability of this large animal with its slowness to comprehend often also caused her to misunderstand his words.

After the fraction of a second when he had experienced fear and weakness, his power over the animals remained in question, and the continually returning experience of powerlessness over his own wife weakened his focus in life from then on. Everything in his soul and his character had been suppressed in favor of the one desire that dominated all else: to exercise power over others without force. The loss of this power left nothing remaining of the once self-confident, powerful, successful man. In the course of one short year he came to realize that he would never succeed in training either her or the animals with the same confidence as before. So he finally sank to the subordinate position of an attendant and stable boy in the circus. The lord and master of the Bengal tiger had become the man who has to clean out his cage.

"I then had no choice but to divorce my wife, although I still loved her just as much as before," said the attendant. "I don't know whether you will comprehend that, Doctor. I'm sure that you've never been in such a situation. A man is permitted to make a sacrifice for a woman, to be sure, but not the sacrifice of his self-respect. At least that's how it seemed to me then. I felt like a demoted general who is supposed to serve as a lieutenant's orderly," the attendant continued with a smile, and even the martial form of the comparison, with its vocabulary from the military domain, let it be known that inwardly he had long since turned his defeat into victory, his humiliation into consolation. "I left the circus and accepted the position as attendant here. I thought that next to these animals that had been abased through inactivity and long confinement I could acquire my sovereignty again. But something else happened. In time it became clear to me that I had previously not really understood the animals at all, and as that understanding came, all of my pride disappeared. For it had been human arrogance to set myself up as the ruler of their instincts, simply because as a human being I could twist my own drives together into a rope of many threads, which was then very strong, of course. As an animal trainer I had put a noose around nature's neck."

"I already said it once!" the doctor cried. "Your training was black magic, sorcery."

"Today I have a completely different attitude toward the animals," the attendant continued calmly. "I know that they are independent from me. They live in a different world than I do. There they are the stronger ones. The moment they are pressed into our world, they probably lose their superiority, and then it's proper for me to help them. It's for me to alleviate somewhat the disaster that we bring over them. Nothing more."

The attendant slowly emptied his glass, placed it on the table, and pushed it hesitantly back and forth for a while. Then he noticeably pulled himself together and directed his gaze resolutely but full of kindness at the physician.

"Since I saw her in the clinic again, it has gradually become clear to me that I didn't love my wife as a man, but also only as an animal trainer."

He paused, then he directed his gaze at the doctor again and continued. "I hope you won't be angry with me, Doctor. Perhaps you too confront her not as an attendant but as an animal trainer. She probably has something about her that invites that. But I believe if you cure Mona Belinda she'll be nothing more than the divorced wife of a circus performer who failed and the current wife of a murderer. In reality, however, she's a Bengal tiger's sweetheart."

"I'm a doctor," said Klingengast kindly. "It's my duty to free her from her delusion."

The attendant nodded several times. "Yes, that's probably true. You must do your duty, Doctor. But you'll fail for the same reason that I failed."

Klingengast remembered the conversation that they had had sometime earlier. "You mean, because there's nothing behind it but emptiness. Absolutely nothing at all. Isn't that what you said?"

The attendant nodded.

"Yes. I still believed that at the time. But now that I've seen her again, I believe that there's a strong idea back there, even in her case. Even if it's a delusion. Perhaps for Mona Belinda the tiger is her god, and she allows herself to be eaten by him, skin, hair, and all. For her, he's the stronger one."

The doctor listened attentively and took it as a sign of their solidifying friendship that superiority or greater knowledge had become trivial between them because each accorded the strange thoughts of the other their rights.

The attendant continued. "Who knows if that which I have become, contrary to my original nature and my vain thirst for power, is not also acting under the constraint of a foreign will, of someone stronger. . ."

"You mean. . . ," but he did not say it aloud.

"When I became acquainted with the boy," the attendant said, "I also only wanted to train him. It was child's play, a test of strength. But now I surrender. I want to make amends for what I did wrong with his mother. I don't want to adopt him to be an animal trainer to him, but a father."

Over the long and intensive conversation, they had not noticed that it had meanwhile become evening. When they stood up, the doctor glanced at the clock and the attendant said, "The zoo is already closed, and the park gates will also no longer be open. Please go left down the street. Meanwhile, I'll get my keys and let you out the back way, at the exit for the zoo personnel."

Klingengast nodded and slowly walked on beneath the silent, ancient chestnut trees, and it seemed to him, after the human conversation had died, as though he could hear nature's grand, soundless monologue again, its quiet existence that rests in itself. Even the animals were asleep, the birds with their heads under their wings, the cats curled up. Only the wolf, an agitated gray shadow, performed its insane dance, three steps down, three steps back, behind the bars. How much he must long for his natural freedom to hunt and be hunted, to mangle, and to be mangled by horrible steel traps! What drove him to it? What was stronger than the advantages of sated security behind limiting and simultaneously protecting bars?

He thought of the bow-legged little sex murderer, and of Mona Belinda, the divided, superhumanly tall woman. What drove them, these people who were spurned by everyone, who stood out from the normal form like rusty nails on a box, whose destiny fell out of the normal order of things—what drove them to let themselves be eaten up, skin, hair, and all, by that destiny?!

And the words "be eaten up" suddenly brought his dream to mind again. So there was something of it even in him. Kept secret. Under the threshold. But still he knew how to bridle it. As a human being in full possession of his moral consciousness, he rose far enough above his own nature to control himself. The animal had become human—into what would it develop in the course of the coming millennia?

For seconds, the possibility of his transcending to higher orders opened within him as a dazzling hope and a deep, incomprehensible insight.

In front of the tiger's cage, he suddenly stopped as though rooted to the ground and felt cold waves of horror streaming to his heart. For there lay the enormous animal on its side with its paws stretched out, in a half-awake predator slumber that was disturbed by quivering reflexes, and pressed against the whitish belly fur, little Josef also lay sleeping peacefully, without any suspicion of the danger in which he hovered.

The doctor was still standing there petrified when the attendant hastily approached.

"My key ring is gone!" he said distraughtly, and then he saw the boy lying between the Bengal tiger's paws.

"Well, go on!" whispered Klingengast. "Go now! You must get him out of there before the animal wakes up!"

The attendant took an uncertain step forward, but then he stopped and answered just as softly, "I can't go in now. I'm afraid, and that's dangerous. They smell it. For them, he who is afraid is guilty."

It was the fear that originated in the past and had broken forth again, that ulcer of an unpaid debt. It was guilt; the animals knew it. They had already known it then, and new guilt had developed from it: the destruction of Mona Belinda's life.

"No, not now," he murmured. "Not again. . . Jesus Christ!" he suddenly added, almost inaudibly.

For the tiger had raised its head and was looking over at the two men. His eyes gleamed pale green in the first twilight of evening. Then he turned his head to the resting figure, sniffed soundlessly, and licked the boy's face caressingly with his long, wet, red tongue. Half asleep, the boy lifted his hand, caught hold of the mouth of the tiger, who tenderly continued to lick him, and pushed it aside in annoyance. Only then did he blinkingly open his eyes. He was still confused with sleep.

The attendant made a gesture with his hand. "Josef!" he called softly.

Now the boy raised his head and straightened up. Suddenly wide awake, he recognized the two men in front of the cage, stood up, and hesitatingly came right up to the bars. With his hands he clasped two of the iron bars in despair and defiance, but his emaciated, dirt-encrusted, aged child's face had a pleading expression. He seemed prepared to entrench himself in this cage against any new effort of the hostile adults, for his father, the Bengal tiger, was there, and he had never before been acquainted with a different, more human fatherliness.

The tiger too had slightly lifted a paw, but that movement was not threatening. The claws remained retracted and the dangerous paw was rolled up into a playful foot. Very silent and lazily watchful, he looked at the two men. Then he calmly began to lick his foot, yawned once briefly, and let himself fall to his side again to go back to sleep.

The attendant let out his breath as slowly and lengthily as if he had been holding it for the whole time.

"Come out, Josef," he said. "You can stay with me. You don't have to go back to the orphanage."

Quick as a flash the little boy let go of the bars and trotted to the door of the cage. Nor did he forget to lock the cage carefully behind him as he had learned from his friend and mentor. Then he ran trustingly to him and gave him the ring of keys.

"Really?" he asked breathlessly. "For certain?"

"Yes," said the attendant. "For as long as you want."

AFTERWORD

It is not difficult to establish relationships between Jeannie Ebner's narratives and the writings of other twentieth-century Austrian authors. The mythological, allegorical, and surrealistic elements in her early works bring to mind Franz Kafka's peculiarly penetrating visions of modern existence, while her later emphasis on rationality and psychological reality parallels Robert Musil's approach to the portrayal of contemporary life. Even more relevant for *The Bengal Tiger*, however, is the mastery of poetic and symbolic expression that links this particular creation to another significant model, the lyric poetry of Rainer Maria Rilke.

Rilke's most important contribution to poetry was the *Dinggedicht*, or object poem. Works of this type examine paintings, pieces of sculpture, landscapes, animals, plants, human figures, structures, and even themes from the Bible and mythology, in attempts to interpret the world and clarify existence in new ways. Among the most famous of Rilke's *Dinggedichte* are "Der Panther" (The Panther), which presents its object as a symbol for a heroic life, and "Das Karussell" (The Merry-Go-Round), a symbolic representation of the world as a whole.

The intent behind Rilke's object poems was penetration to the basic essence of things and relationships by reducing them to elements in an absolute realm of pure symbol. In that context, understanding of the symbols could then lead to comprehension of the phenomena that they represented. To that extent, it might be argued that *The Bengal Tiger* is an example of the logical expansion, adaptation, and employment of Rilke's *Dinggedicht* principle in a prose narrative. Moreover, the parallels between Rilke's symbolic panther and carousel on the one hand and Ebner's tiger and traveling circus on the other almost suggest that the object poems actually provided models, or at least productive stimuli for significant elements in Ebner's story.

The caged panther of Rilke's poem has several important characteristics. It is described as weary and indifferent to what lies beyond the bars; it lives in its own private world. At the same time, it is the embodiment of focused power, of a strong, albeit torpid will. Finally, it has the ability to draw the outside world into itself—in this case, through its gaze—and to determine the destiny of what it sees.

Although a different animal, Ebner's Bengal tiger is remarkably similar to the panther. It too is portrayed as tired and apathetic toward the outside world, its will and instincts all but deadened by prolonged captivity. Significantly, the great insight that the zoo keeper's extended association with the predator cat has given him is that the tiger really lives in a different world where it is the stronger being, the master. The attendant has gained that knowledge in part through a tragic experience in which he failed to maintain control over the animal through the exercise of his own will, and he has come to the realization that it was wrong to attempt to impose his will on the tiger in the first place.

The most important dimension of the tiger's symbolic nature is its power to shape the destinies of people in the world outside. Like Rilke's panther, it figuratively draws in elements from the domain beyond its cage and consumes or transforms them. Dr. Klingengast dreams about begging the tiger to eat him, and in the closed-off inner life of her insanity, Mona Belinda, whose beauty the tiger has forever marred, yields herself completely to the tiger's will and longs to be eaten by her ferocious lover. The boy is unceasingly drawn to the huge animal in a similar but less destructive way. Unlike his mother, little Josef views the tiger as a protective rather than a consumptive force. In his mind he longs to enter the refuge of the big cat's separate world and be acknowledged by a loving and powerful father as the tiger's son.

Confrontations with the tiger affect the other characters in different ways. For Anna, little Josef's grandmother, the tiger is the embodiment of the demonic force against which she must struggle all her life in order not to be consumed. For her son-in-law, the unknown "stronger one" who disfigured his wife represents despair and the other unseen enemies against which he does not have the strength to fight, forces that ultimately transform him into a sex-murderer. And for the former animal trainer, the tiger is the personification of nature who changes him from master to servant. In each case, encounter with the tiger is critical experience with life as it is or as it must become for the person involved.

While Rilke's panther and Ebner's tiger are symbols for the life of the individual, the carousel and the circus denote life in a broader sense, as it encompasses the history of mankind. Again there are visible similarities between the creations of the two writers.

Rilke's merry-go-round is a world in endless movement, filled with animals, people, colors. The procession goes on and on in circles, without a visible goal. Impressions of life flash by the spectator's eyes, one after another, as in a blind and breathless game.

Like the carousel, Ebner's circus symbolizes life in motion. At one point in the story, Anna, the grandmother, even equates her existence with an endless stream of changing impressions that flash past like the parts of a circus parade. But where Rilke's poem emphasizes the visual experience of people and things seen on the merry-go-round, Ebner's story derives its power from the detailed presentation of the characters' direct interaction with elements of the circus.

As an extremely complex symbol for mortal existence in general, Ebner's circus is primarily employed as a context for the depiction of timeless human conflicts. For example, the portion of the narrative that presents the animal trainer's failure to maintain dominion over the tiger becomes an allegory for the problem of the tension between man and nature that can only be resolved when man accepts his true role as nature's steward and not its controller. Similarly, the collapse of the act portraying the Garden of Eden is an ironic representation of man's fall from innocence and the subsequent disharmony between male and female. Other important themes that are treated include the clashing wills of parent and child, the polarities of freedom and confinement, light and darkness, ugliness and beauty, and the loss of a feeling of social responsibility.

In many respects, *The Bengal Tiger* in its entirety can be viewed as a detailed poetic documentation of the vain human struggle to regain harmony with the world after the loss of innocence. In addition to the tragic events in the circus ring that destroy the animal trainer's career, the motifs of the serpent's destructive temptation of Adam and Eve are presented in several other variations involving the contact of "spectators" with representatives of the circus. For the young Anna, the serpent is the well-dressed, handsome circus magician, who symbolically drops the red apple into her basket and eventually seduces her. The father of little Josef Kutian is captivated by the red, serpentine scar left by the tiger on the former Eve's cheek and neck and is lured into a destructive relationship that eventually transforms him into a sex-murderer. Even the boy assumes the role of the serpent when he attempts to use an apple to lure his mother from the private world of animal innocence to which her insanity has confined her.

By giving her distinctly poetic inclinations free rein in the creation of *The Bengal Tiger*, Jeannie Ebner accomplished in the prose narrative what Rainer Maria Rilke desired to achieve with his *Dinggedichte*: a new interpretation of the world in powerful symbols. The conventions of prose enabled her to give the symbols greater depth and meaning than was possible in lyric poetry, while permitting her to explore real human problems in significant detail. To that extent, *The Bengal Tiger* can perhaps best be described as an extremely compelling *Dinggeschichte*, or object story.

ARIADNE PRESS

Studies in Austrian Literature, Culture and Thought

*Major Figures of
Modern Austrian Literature*
Edited by
Donald G. Daviau

*Major Figures of
Turn-of-the-Century
Austrian Literature*
Edited by Donald G. Daviau

*Austrian Writers and the
Anschluss: Understanding the
Past—Overcoming the Past*
Edited by Donald G. Daviau

*Introducing Austria
A Short History*
By Lonnie Johnson

*Coexistent Contradictions
Joseph Roth in Retrospect*
Edited by
Helen Chambers

*The Verbal and Visual Art of
Alfred Kubin*
By Phillip H. Rhein

*Kafka and Language
In the Stream of
Thoughts and Life*
By G. von Natzmer Cooper

*Robert Musil and the Tradition
of the German Novelle*
By Kathleen O'Connor

*Austria in the Thirties
Culture and Politics*
Edited by Kenneth Segar
and John Warren

*Stefan Zweig:
An International Bibliography*
By Randolph J. Klawiter

*Austrian Foreign Policy
Yearbook*
Report of the Austrian Federal
Ministry for Foreign Affairs
for the Year 1990

*Quietude and Quest
Protagonists and Antagonists in
the Theater, on and off Stage
As Seen Through the Eyes of
Leon Askin*
Leon Askin and C. Melvin Davidsor

*"What People Call Pessimism":
Sigmund Freud, Arthur Schnitzler
and Nineteenth-Century
Controversy at the University
of Vienna Medical School*
By Mark Luprecht

Arthur Schnitzler and Politics
By Adrian Clive Roberts

*Structures of Disintegration
Narrative Strategies in
Elias Canetti's* Die Blendung
By David Darby

ARIADNE PRESS

Translation Series:

February Shadows
By Elisabeth Reichart
Translated by Donna L. Hoffmeister
Afterword by Christa Wolf

Night Over Vienna
By Lili Körber
Translated by Viktoria Hertling
and Kay M. Stone. Commentary
by Viktoria Hertling

The Cool Million
By Erich Wolfgang Skwara
Translated by Harvey I. Dunkle
Preface by Martin Walser
Afterword by Richard Exner

Buried in the Sands of Time
Poetry by Janko Ferk
English/German/Slovenian
English Translation
by Herbert Kuhner

Puntigam or The Art of Forgetting
By Gerald Szyszkowitz
Translated by Adrian Del Caro
Preface by Simon Wiesenthal
Afterword by Jürgen Koppensteiner

Negatives of My Father
By Peter Henisch
Translated and with an Afterword
by Anne C. Ulmer

On the Other Side
By Gerald Szyszkowitz
Translated by Todd C. Hanlin
Afterword by Jürgen Koppensteiner

*I Want to Speak
The Tragedy and Banality
of Survival in
Terezin and Auschwitz*
By Margareta Glas-Larsson
Edited and with a Commentary
by Gerhard Botz
Translated by Lowell A. Bangerter

The Works of Solitude
By György Sebestyén
Translated and with an
Afterword by
Michael Mitchell

Remembering Gardens
By Kurt Klinger
Translated by Harvey I. Dunkle

Deserter
By Anton Fuchs
Translated and with an Afterword
by Todd C. Hanlin

From Here to There
By Peter Rosei
Translated and with an Afterword
by Kathleen Thorpe

The Angel of the West Window
By Gustav Meyrink
Translated by Michael Mitchell

*Relationships
An Anthology of Contemporary
Austrian Literature*
Selected and with an Introduction
by Adolf Opel